JANET K. SHAWGO

It's for the Best

Merry Christmas Betty

Sincerely Janet Shawgo

Five Ladi

First edition

ISBN: 978-1-7334045-2-5

Cover art by Michelle Rene
Proofreading by Diane Garland
Editing by Joan Acklin

This book was professionally typeset on Reedsy.
Find out more at reedsy.com

"To good friends and cold beer!"

Contents

II Time Forward

I

The Past

Chapter 1

1936

Lillie Glenmore opened the oven and removed a pan of biscuits placing it on a hot pad. Using her fingers to pick them up, they were put into a small basket lined with a blue flowered napkin. With a quick swipe of her hands on the yellow apron covering the housedress, she took the basket and a jam bowl to the table. A full day's work in the Texas summer heat was ahead. She noticed her daughter seemed to be more interested in the chickens outside instead of breakfast. Times had changed from her braiding Gean's hair like a child's, to now discussing matters of a maturing young woman.

"Gean, is there something wrong?"

"No mother, why?" Gean asked turning her head back towards Lillie.

"I've never known you to not like my jams. I did make apricot, your favorite."

"I'm not very hungry this morning, mother."

"Do you not feel well?" Lillie asked reaching out to feel Gean's head.

"I'm not ill."

"What's wrong, Gean?"

"Mother, I'm no longer comfortable going with dad to force money from people who do not have it to give. What we are doing is wrong."

From the first day Gean left the house with Ambrose, Lillie knew this moment would eventually come. Reaching out taking her daughter's hand would be the only outward support she would be allowed to give.

3

"You haven't spoken with your father have you?"

"No. Mother, but I can't continue to look into the eyes of our neighbors knowing they fear us."

Ambrose Glenmore had taken Gean with him to collect debts before she could walk. She began to respond when he appeared in the doorway ending their conversation. Releasing Gean's hand watching as he lit a cigarette taking a long draw blowing smoke towards them.

"Gean, where is your ledger?" he asked.

"In my room."

"How will I know who is behind on their debts? Go get it," he said.

Gean nodded and left the table.

Lillie waited until she was out of hearing, stood facing her husband. "Ambrose, you need to give Gean the option to go with you. She's no longer a child. In a few weeks, she will be sixteen, old enough to make her own choices."

"I'm not going to have this conversation with you, woman. The fact she is no longer a child makes these trips even more important."

"Important for who?" Lillie asked. Footsteps in the hallway ceased their conversation for the moment.

"I'm ready," Gean said.

"Go get in the car."

"Yes, sir."

Lillie smiled at her daughter and nodded.

Ambrose walked over to the table extinguishing his cigarette in the small container of jam.

"Woman, stay out of my business. If it weren't for the money I collect, Gean would be going to school with the local trash. You don't have a problem spending my money on your clothes or this house. Don't involve yourself with things you do not understand." He walked to the back door taking his fedora off the hat stand.

Following him to the door Lillie watched as he stood adjusting his hat. Ambrose was a big man. His height and weight only added to his demeanor when collecting a debt. She waved to Gean as they drove away from the house.

Clearing the uneaten food from the table she frowned at the cigarette in her jam bowl. Ambrose was disappointed when she gave birth to a girl. He gave their daughter a man's name and began to plan her future. There was never any consideration to what their daughter might want one day. Ambrose Glenmore intended to have a legacy, but at what cost? If he continued to push, Gean would eventually push back one day.

Ambrose drove towards the city occasionally glancing towards his daughter. He was worried his wife was working against him and Gean's future. He had not come this far in life by being soft. There was only one thing people understood when it came to money, a stern voice and hard fist. It was a difficult time for the people of Glenmore. Debts must be paid regardless of the economic difficulties and many needed reminding.

He was fortunate to obtain the obscene amount of land in the panhandle of Texas. Ambrose's plan from the very beginning was to form the city of Glenmore. This included promises of land and financial assistance to anyone who would move to his town. Families and businesses would be encouraged to borrow money directly from him. The contracts people signed promised payments in good or bad times. If the debt went unpaid he would force them out. Losing nothing and caring less for the lives that were ruined.

There had been many rumors in the town as to the means Ambrose used to obtain the land. It was said he won it in an unfair poker game. Another story indicated the town was built on blood. A smile crossed his face as both stories caused fear in the eyes of those he met on the street.

"Gean, who is the first person we need to collect from this morning?" He waited for an answer. Ambrose glanced towards his daughter who hadn't opened her ledger. "Gean!"

She jumped in the seat and turned towards him.

"I'm sorry, what did you say?"

"Pay attention! Open your ledger, who is behind on their payments? What is wrong with you this morning?"

Gean took a deep breath. "Dad, why is it necessary for us to treat people we know so badly?"

"Loaning money is a business, it's not about friends. You should understand this by now."

"I understand we are fortunate to have money for loans. There are times when kindness and understanding are necessary."

"Kindness and understanding don't pay for your school or put the clothes on your back. I will not be cheated out of my money," he said.

"It doesn't mean anyone is trying to cheat you. They may need extra time to pay. Dad, these people are our neighbors, many of them my friends, who have fallen on tough times. It's difficult for me to see us take what little they have especially when we don't need the money."

Ambrose's face turned red. He could not believe the words coming from his daughter. Pulling to the side of the road and stopping the car abruptly he changed positions in the car. Facing her he pointed his finger in her face.

"Who have you been talking to? Leroy Grinder? The pastor at the Baptist church? The teachers at your fancy school? Or maybe your mother has been putting these thoughts in your head!"

Gean shook her head. "No one has been talking to me about what is right or wrong. I have a mind of my own. I can think..."

"Who told you to think? Don't think! Watch, listen, and learn what it means to have a business."

Gean didn't answer.

"Gean! You will answer when I ask you a question."

"Yes, sir."

"Good, you will pay attention today. People do not respond to kindness or mercy. Those traits are a weakness, it allows people to cheat you. In my absence, you will be expected to collect and deal with debtors as I do. This means demanding money on time or they pay the penalty. There will be no exceptions! You are a Glenmore act like it!"

Chapter 2

Sparks

Leroy Grinder, removed his hat wiping the sweat from his brow as he drove into town. His dark brown hair was wet from the long drive on a hot day. He prayed the Farmer's Almanac was wrong in regards to the long Texas summer to come. The Circle G ranch was not the largest in the area but he could not afford to lose any cattle, it would ruin him. He drove past the J&M local drive-in. Jacob and Millie were sitting outside at one of the picnic tables. He would stop later for a cold soda and a piece of Millie's homemade pie once the supplies were loaded.

Pulling the pickup into the dirt lot of Blake and Sons feed store he could see Gean Glenmore at the top of the steps. He turned to speak to his ranch hand, Bo Hackney. The young man caught sight of the lovely young girl at the top of the steps. Leroy understood the young man's interest, but being the daughter of the richest man in town had drawbacks.

"Bo, I need you to load the feed."

The young man didn't respond.

"Bo!"

"Yes sir."

"Please load the feed. If you hurry we'll stop at the restaurant before going back to the ranch," Leroy told him.

"I will, Mr. Grinder. I love the pie there."

"What is it, Bo?"

"Who is that girl? I've never seen her."

"Her name is Gean, the daughter of Ambrose Glenmore. He owns and runs pretty much the entire town."

"Why haven't I seen her in school?"

Leroy laughed. "Ambrose can't have his darling daughter go to school with the peasants. She goes to a fancy boarding school up North."

"She's cute."

Leroy took a moment before he spoke.

"Bo, I would suggest you keep your distance."

The boy nodded and left the truck.

Bo was sixteen and living at the Circle G Ranch since he was thirteen. Leroy discovered the young boy in his barn, cold and hungry. The few words the boy spoke indicated his home was in Dalhart and a name Bo Hackney. Contacting the sheriff in town he reported there was a possible runaway at the ranch. A week later the sheriff visited to the Circle G. He would never forget the conversation.

"Leroy, I contacted the sheriff over in Dalhart. This boy has not been reported missing by his family."

"What type of folks are they?"

"The sheriff up there said his father was a mean old bastard. Enjoyed beating his wife and Bo."

"I suspected something like that with all the bruises on him. No kind of life for a young boy."

"What are you going to do with him?" The sheriff asked.

"Turning him out it pretty much guarantees a life of thievery, jail time, or loss of life. If he stays here, helping me, there's a chance to prove kind people exist in the world."

Bo Hackney remained on the Circle G. ranch with Leroy becoming like a son. The young man worked hard in school and on the ranch. In return clothes, food, and a warm place to sleep were provided.

Gean smiled as he reached the top of the stairs. "Good morning, Mr. Grinder."

"Good morning, Gean. Is your father here?"

She frowned. "Yes, sir."

Placing his hand on her shoulder. "You stay out here."

She nodded walking down the stairs.

Leroy entered the feed store where a loud unnecessary conversation was taking place between Ambrose and Tom Blake. It ended with Tom removing twenty dollars from the cash drawer handing it to Ambrose.

"Try to be on time next month Tom," Ambrose said, turning almost running into Leroy.

"Ambrose, there is no need for you to scream at people, especially in their own business. I don't understand why you are still forcing Gean to follow you around town collecting your blood money?"

Ambrose laughed. "She needs to see how it is in the real world of men. Gean!"

"I asked her to remain outside. I don't believe she needs to learn it's better to take from those who have little, giving it to someone who has everything," Leroy said.

"Debt is debt. Where would I be if I gave money away? I see no issue with her becoming..."

"A ruthless, heartless piece of shit like her father. You have the money and influence to do a lot of good for the people of this town. Instead, you bully and take, caring nothing for the damage you do to others, including Gean," Leroy said.

Ambrose walked up to Leroy and poked him in the chest. "I don't remember you having an issue with my methods when I removed the squatters off the land you wanted."

He looked towards Tom Blake then faced Ambrose. "Leave your daughter at home. Give her a chance to have the life she chooses."

"My daughter's life is none of your business."

Leroy pushed past Ambrose, walking over to pay for his supplies. They were the same height, around six foot three. Over the years Ambrose gained too much weight adding to his bullying manner. He exited the feed store, holding back to observe an interesting scene taking place. Gean was sitting on the tailgate of his truck laughing with Bo. He leaned against the rail as the screen door slammed behind him.

"Gean!"

"Yes, Dad," she said.

"Come here."

Jumping off the tailgate Gean straightened her skirt then ran up the steps. Leroy motioned for Bo to load another bag of feed. He turned to see Ambrose grab Gean by the arm.

"What did I tell you about the trash?" Ambrose asked.

"Dad!" She pulled away.

"You are not dressed appropriately to sit on the tailgate of a truck. We need to leave, go get in the car."

Leroy shook his head.

"Ambrose, Bo Hackney is not trash. He is a hard worker has high marks in school and left a bad home situation. I intend to give him the opportunity for a better life."

"I don't give a damn what you do with him. He'll never be good enough to do anything except scrape the dirt off my daughter's shoes," Ambrose said. Walking away only to turn around and point his finger at Leroy. "Keep him away from her!"

Gean rolled down the window and waved as they drove away. Leroy had been around Gean since she was old enough to walk. He could see she was beginning to disapprove of her father's business practices. Most folks discovered too late the consequences of borrowing money from Ambrose. The attempt to mold Gean in his image was starting to fall apart. One day she would rebel. Hopefully, he would be around to see it. He walked down to the pickup.

"Bo!"

"Yes, sir."

"What were you two talking about?"

"Not much. She wanted to know if I lived around here, my age, how I liked the school. That's all, honest Mr. Grinder."

Leroy knew from the moment he saw them talking there was a spark. There were two choices, allow Gean to become another Ambrose or fan the flames of young love.

"Bo, I can't keep you from talking to Gean especially when we happen to be in the same location. I would suggest you not speak if her father is present."

Bo smiled. "Yes, sir."

Chapter 3

June 1938

  Circle G.

Bo Hackney was up before sunrise to begin his chores at the ranch. Mr. Grinder was going to allow him to drive into town alone today for the ranch supplies. Reaching in his back jean pocket he pulled out a letter. The words were beginning to fade as it was read every day for the last month. The little hearts drawn around his name brought a smile. Today Gean was coming home for the summer.

Over the last two summers, they became good friends, writing while she was at school and managing to meet up with friends in the town. He had been careful to heed Mr. Grinder's warning not speak or look Gean's way when Mr. Glenmore was with her. Close friends became complicit in their growing relationship, covering for them to sneak away for sunset picnics or a movie in Amarillo. Last summer he finally asked if she would be his girl. Secrets were not easy in Glenmore, but they managed to keep their relationship from her dad.

"You're up awful early this morning, Bo," Leroy said.

"Yes, sir. I wanted to be caught up on the chores. I don't wish to be working after dark, since I'm heading into town for supplies today."

Leroy smiled. "Are you sure it isn't because Gean's going to be there?"

Bo's face turned red. "I want to see how she is doing."

"I would have thought all those letters I've been picking up at the post office for you would have explained her health."

Bo kicked the dirt. "I..."

"I need you to get the feed out to the animals, check the south fence and come back. If I were you, I'd clean up, before heading into town to see Gean. She won't take kindly to you smelling like the cows. Is she meeting you at the feed store?"

"No. At J&M, with Billie and Florence."

Leroy shook his head. "Florence Bigalow is a good girl. You need to be careful around Wilhelmina."

"Who is Wilhelmina?"

"I should have said, Billie. Wilhelmina is Billie Dwyer's given name. She comes from a good family of hard workers. The girl has a streak of envy running through her for those with more. The girl's desires are higher than her daddy can afford. I believe it is one reason she hangs around Gean."

Bo stood for a moment. "I don't like to speak out of turn."

"Spit it out, what have you heard?" Leroy asked.

"I've heard Billie speak badly of folks with less than her. She never seems to have any money when Gean's around. I've seen her paying for things, " Bo said.

"What type of things?"

"I've seen Gean buy food at J&M's for her, candy at the feed store. I know she bought Billie an expensive hair scarf at Miss Anne's dress shop last year."

"Did Gean buy anything for Florence?"

"Florence is never around when Gean pays."

Leroy frowned. "She's taking advantage of her good heart and knows the Glenmore's have money. It doesn't seem to bother Billie to spend Gean's money."

"Florence and Billie are considered to be Gean's best friends. Do you think I should say something to her?" Bo said.

"I'm going to give a little adult and manly advice. If it doesn't involve you, stay out of women's business. Gean's a bright girl and will eventually figure out what Billie's doing," Leroy said.

Chapter 4

J&M Drive-in

Billie Dwyer waited outside the drive-in at one of the old wooden picnic tables. She arrived early to make sure they had one of the two tables under a large shade tree. Giving her friend, Florence, the wrong time to meet there to have a private conversation with Gean. A horn honk caused Billie to turn and see Gean in her daddy's Cadillac. It must be nice to drive a new car instead of walking or riding a bicycle as she was forced to do in the Texas sun. As Gean exited the car Billie forced a smile.

"Did you order?"

"No. Could you get me a cherry lime?" Billie asked.

"Sure, I'll get one for Flo," Gean said.

"She is going to be a little late," Billie said.

"I'll have Millie hold it until she gets here."

Billie rolled her eyes as Gean walked away. Always Miss Goodie Two Shoes. It was difficult to watch as she wore new clothes from a fancy store up north. Going to some uppity school, flaunting daddy's money forced out of the pockets of poor folks like her parents. One day, she would have money and wear the same expensive clothes just like her friend. Gean returned with drinks.

"Thanks," Billie said.

Gean sat down. "I want to go over the plan for today."

"I think we can handle it, Gean. We've done this for what two years now? Flo and I will take your daddy's car to Amarillo, stay for three hours. We'll meet you and Bo later at the Holiday Movie Drive-In."

"I don't know what I would do without my best friends. The car is full of gas. Don't fill it up in case my dad checks." Gean said.

"What about..." Billie said, holding out an empty hand.

"Oh, sorry. I'm so excited to see Bo I forgot." Gean opened her purse, handing Billie the keys to the Cadillac and a ten-dollar bill.

Billie smiled. "I'd keep your secret for nothing."

"I know," Gean said wrapping an arm around Billie.

"Your thoughtfulness is appreciated," Billie said.

"I thought you and Flo could go to a movie or shop. Robin Hood is playing in Amarillo. Errol Flynn is so handsome and dreamy, go see that one."

Bo pulled into the J&M the same time Flo arrived on her bicycle. Gean waved at both of them.

"Have you been here long?" Flo asked.

"Long enough to buy you a cold soda. Millie will get it for you anytime," Gean told her.

"Thank you." Flo walked to the window to get the drink.

"Are you ready to go?" Bo asked.

Gean nodded turning back to Billie. "See you in three hours."

"See you two at the drive-in." She watched them leave placing the ten dollars in her dress pocket.

Flo joined Billie at the table.

"Where are we going today?" Flo asked.

"Unless you brought a couple of dollars not far," Billie answered.

"I have three dollars."

"We can go to the movie get a hamburger afterward," Billie said.

"Or maybe we can get him to go with us and I won't have to spend my money," Flo said jumping up from the table. She was halfway across the parking lot before Billie even had a chance to stand up.

"Bitch," she said making sure no one heard the comment.

First, it was Gean and Bo, now Flo was throwing herself at Jackson Hellman. He was older, handsome, and committed to finishing college. Billie knew Jackson would be someone important one day. The heat was rising in her face as Flo took Jackson's hand and returned to the table. Jackson and Bo were the two best-looking men in town.

The only person who compared to them would be Amos Walsh. She shivered. The Walsh family owned a large successful farming equipment business in Glenmore. Amos tried several times in school to court her. If he'd lose a little weight she might consider it.

"Billie, guess what," Flo said.

"I can't imagine," Billie said.

"Jackson has offered to take the three of us to Amarillo for the afternoon."

"That's wonderful, but I need to take Gean's car and follow Jackson. This way should you two wish to stay longer it won't interfere with me returning the car."

Flo looked up at Jackson. "I..."

"Flo, seriously, go enjoy the rest of the day together. I have some things I can do here in Glenmore. Have a nice afternoon," Billie told her.

"Are you sure?"

"I'm sure."

"I'll talk to you later," Flo said.

Watching the two walk away Billie removed the ten-dollar bill from her pocket. "I have plans for you at Miss Anne's.

Chapter 5

Proposal

Bo drove out to a spot of land with a small canyon at the back of the property to show Gean. He discovered this property six months ago and began to check for an owner and possible sale price. Due to his age, the clerk at the courthouse wasn't helpful.

One evening he discussed the interest in purchasing the land with Mr. Grinder. A detailed plan for cattle and oil exploration once purchased was discussed. Once the two walked the property, he agreed to help Bo. Mr. Grinder obtained the information and was instrumental in obtaining a fair price for the property.

"Bo, this is pretty back here by the canyon," she said.

"I found this a while back and thought you might enjoy the view."

"It's lovely."

"I'm glad you like it because I put money down to buy it."

"Did you show it to Mr. Grinder?"

"He helped me," Bo said.

Smiling at him. "Congratulations, landowner."

"Not yet, in another year it will be mine."

They left the pickup. Bo took Gean's hand walking around showing where he wanted to build a house, the barn, and plant a garden.

"It appears you have everything figured out," she said.

"Not everything. I'm going to need help," he said nervously.

"Are you asking me to help you?"

Bo's face turned red. "I was hoping you might marry me one day."

"Marry you and live out here?"

He wasn't sure what to say next. Did she think he was ridiculous? Bo didn't know what to make of the last comment.

"I'm sorry, I shouldn't..."

Gean couldn't hold the laughter any longer. "Yes. I will marry you one day. We will live out here on this beautiful land and raise a family. There is one request."

"Anything you want," he said.

"The porch must face the canyon."

Bo grabbed Gean around the waist, hugging and kissing her. The next hour they sat on the tailgate of the truck making plans for the future.

"I convinced my father to let me stay home and go to college in Amarillo."

"How?"

"Simple. I explained staying close would allow me the opportunity to become seriously involved with the business."

"Isn't the college a two-year program?"

She nodded. "We'll need to do something before he tries to send me away to finish my educations.

"Two years seems like a long time."

"It's not, time will go quick. I have an idea, but it will take the people we trust to succeed."

"Mr. Grinder," he said.

"And my mother. She will do whatever it takes for me to be safe and happy."

"I love you, Gean. I'll show Mr. Glenmore one day I'm a good person."

"It doesn't matter what my father thinks. I know you are a good hard-working decent person. I love you." Gean leaned over kissing him.

"We should head back into town. I don't want to give your father a reason to start questioning you," Bo said.

The drive back was quiet. Bo placed his right arm around Gean sitting next to him on the bench seat, her head on his shoulder. This was the way he always wanted them to be. Pulling into the empty lot he parked in a corner. This way they could see anyone coming towards them. Bo turned off the motor.

"I want to talk to you before Billie gets here," he said.

"Is something wrong?"

"Gean, please don't say anything..."

She touched his arm pointing out the windshield. "Tell me quickly, she's early."

"I'm worried. Our future depends on secrecy.If Mr. Glenmore finds out you'll be sent away," he said.

"Oh, there is no need to worry. As long as I continue to pay her to keep quiet things will be fine," she said.

His mouth dropped open. "You know?"

"Billie is a good friend. I have known for a while the only thing in her life which matters is money. She would never say anything to my father if it meant I'd stop funding her trips to Amarillo or Miss Anne's."

"What about Flo?"

"Flo will never say anything. Our friendship means more than money."

Billie walked up to the truck. "Did you two have a nice afternoon?"

"We did. Where is Flo?" Gean asked.

"Flo and Jackson Hellman left right after you. I think they are spending the day in Amarillo. We spent the day shopping in town, where you bought dinner for us at J&M before driving me home."

"Guess we need to head back to J&M," she said, winking at Bo.

"You can get us something to go. I don't want to sit outside with the bugs this evening," Billie said.

Gean kissed Bo on the cheek. "I'll see you in a few days."

Bo opened the door allowing Gean to slide out on the driver's side. He walked them to the car. As she drove away he remained standing in the empty lot for a moment.

Raising both arms in the air. "She said, Yes!"

Chapter 6

Escape

1940, Wednesday

Lillie stood in the yard feeding the chickens on a beautiful cloudless morning. She would always remember this day for the rest of her life. The blue- flowered housedress with a solid blue apron to match had a crispness to them. Taking extra time today to brush her hair a few extra strokes noticing there was more grey these days. The long braid was wrapped and pinned at the base of her neck. She thought of wearing a pair of earrings but feared Ambrose would make a note and ask why.

It had been a year since Bo arrived one evening while Ambrose and Gean were away on business. He knocked on the door, asking politely if he could come in to visit. She remembered his hands shaking as he presented the bouquet of hand-picked sunflowers and her favorite blueberry pie. She knew Leroy told him the flavor of pie to buy at J&M. The bottom of the box was still warm and the smell of Millie's crumble crust permeated the air. Staring at his boots seemed to be the only way to speak to her without stammering.

"Let's cut this pie and have some coffee," she said.

"Yes ma'am. I'd think that would be nice," Bo said.

"I think the kitchen might be a place we can talk."

Bo only nodded she remembered following her like a puppy. After the second piece of pie, he calmed down enough to put a full sentence together.

"Mrs. Glenmore, ma'am, I..." he stopped swallowing hard, taking another sip of coffee.

Lillie smiled hoping it would make his next words easier. "It's fine Bo, speak from your heart."

"I love Gean, pretty much since the first day I saw her at the feed store. The days ahead of us won't always be easy, but I'll make sure she has food and a home. I promise to love her every day until my last breath on this earth. Please say she can marry me. Guess that's all," he said.

Bo's words were touching and sincere which brought tears to her eyes. The moment she took his hand and said yes, the deceit would begin. The only two people who could help them now were her and Leroy.

The hard slam of the screen door brought Lillie back to the stark reality of the present situation. Turning towards Ambrose who stood at the top of the steps searching for Gean. He placed the fedora on walking down the stairs straight to the Cadillac with a small suitcase.

She hid a smile continuing to feed the hens. A simple mistake in the working of a contract was making it possible for Gean to escape. Lillie tightened the grip on the feed pan as he began walking towards her. It was now the time for strength and to play her part. Gean's happiness was at stake. Calling to the chickens she threw a handful of feed.

"Where is Gean?"

"In bed." She answered to the hens.

"Damn!" He turned walking back towards the house.

"Ambrose, stop!" Moving quickly to face him.

"What is it, woman?"

"It's Gean's time of the month. The first day is always bad for her."

He took the fedora off slapping against his leg. "Damn you women and the curse! I need her to go with me. Can't you do something?"

"Ambrose, I'm not a doctor. You will have to go without her."

"This means I'll have to come back here early tomorrow for her to read through the contract. This is damn inconvenient. Doesn't she understand I don't need this type of delay? There is a lot of money to be made and I will not be cheated by some misspelled word or unclear sentence."

"Some mint tea will help but today she needs to rest. Tomorrow will be a better day."

Lillie moved away heading back into the yards. The heavy footsteps could be heard making their way to the car. The wheels were spun driving away in a dust cloud throwing rocks behind. Her heart pounded, praying the lies worked because today was special. Gean and Bo would be married with the help of Leroy Grinder and a few good people in Glenmore. Startled when the screen door opened before the dust cleared.

Gean stuck her head out. "Is he gone?"

Lillie waved a hand. "Get back inside!"

Ambrose would from time to time circle back for one reason or another. He was also the type of man who would change directions driving directly into a storm if meant saving time. They had to be sure he was gone. A few minutes later satisfied he wasn't coming back she placed the feed pan on the ground hurrying inside.

The sight of her daughter made Lillie take a handkerchief from the pocket of the apron dabbing both eyes. Gean stood in the grey Sunday suit and new shoes. Her shoulder-length chestnut hair was curled, held back with a small cloth headband to match the suit.

"Mama please don't cry."

"I'll try sweetheart. Did you remember to leave some of your clothes?" Lillie asked.

"Yes. It won't make any difference. He'll know when I'm not here in the morning," Gean said.

"What about your ledger?" Lillie asked.

"In my suitcase."

"Good, don't ever lose it. Where is the letter?" Lillie asked.

Gean reached for her purse but stopped when the screen door opened. They both jerked around grabbing each other as Bo entered the house. They relaxed releasing their hold. Lillie smiled as Gean's eyes sparkled at her soon-to-be husband. He was dressed in what appeared to be a new pair of jeans, a freshly ironed white shirt, bolo tie, and polished black boots.

"Bo, I hope he didn't see you. He hasn't been gone long," Lillie said.

"I hid down by the curve behind two big trees. When the car was out of view I knew it was safe to leave," Bo's hands were shaking as he held out a small box.

Smiling. "What's this?" Gean asked.

"Every bride needs flowers."

Lillie took the box opening it. She removed a small corsage of pink and white carnations with small sprigs of Lilly of the Valley. Pinning it to her daughter's lapel she pushed back the tears.

"Thank you, Bo. This was very thoughtful," Lillie said.

"Mr. Grinder had me get them. He said it was important."

Lillie smiled. "Leroy is right."

"Are you ready to go?" he asked.

She nodded and turned to her mother. "Please, please go with us to the Circle G."

Lillie hugged and kissed her daughter. "I can't and you know why. It will be easier for me to explain with the letter. If he discovers I was present or helped you in any way...you understand."

Gean picked up the matching purse to the Sunday suit. A letter was removed and given to Lillie. Bo picked up the suitcase opening the screen door. She followed them outside, watching him open the door for her daughter.

"Bo, get as far away from here as possible and stay gone for a while. Don't let Ambrose find her. You hear me?"

He ran up the stairs hugging Lillie. "Yes, ma'am I promise. Thank you."

"Go on now, the preacher will be waiting."

Lillie walked down the stairs standing until the pickup could no longer be seen or heard. When the dust settled she sat down on the steps. The tears running down her face were of joy and relief. Her baby girl was finally safe and in loving arms.

Chapter 7

Truth

Thursday morning

Leroy walked out on the front porch of his new home drinking a morning cup of coffee. It had taken over a year to complete it. Bo and the new ranch hands made it possible to finish ahead of the upcoming branding time. The old home was now a comfortable bunkhouse for the increasing number of cowboys. He built it facing east to enjoy the sunrises and occasional panhandle breeze.

Leaning against the railing of the steps he began to smile. The two cars racing towards the house whipped up a couple of dust devils behind them. The 1940 black Cadillac stopped abruptly with the sheriff's car attempting to catch up. Leroy was surprised the siren wasn't being used with the circling single red light on the county vehicle. The door of the Cadillac swung open with Ambrose jumping out.

Peering down from the top porch at him. "You're going to get that new car of yours dirty coming out here in such a hurry. What can I do for you this morning, Ambrose?"

"You son-of-a-bitch! Where is she? You know! You know where he took her! Tell me, damn you!"

Sheriff Morgan opened the door of his car running up to Ambrose. "Calm down."

Ambrose broke free turning towards him. Pointing up at Leroy. "He knows sheriff, the bastard knows! Tell me, Leroy where is she? Where is my daughter?"

Leroy took a slow drink from the cup still steaming then scratched the back of his head. "You mean Mrs. Hackney."

Ambrose's face turned purple with rage. "I'll kill him! I'll kill him!"

"You're not going to kill anyone," Sheriff Morgan said stepping in front of Ambrose. He looked up at Leroy. "Do you know where they went?"

"God's honest truth, sheriff, I don't have any idea."

"Liar! You did this, you helped him!" Ambrose continued to scream.

"Ambrose has filed a kidnapping report against Bo," Sheriff Morgan said.

Leroy began to laugh in his deep rich voice. "You might want to speak with Pastor Jones about that sheriff. He married them here at the house yesterday. You and I both know the pastor."

"I do. He's a good man. Never know him to do anything outside the church doctrine or against the law," the sheriff said.

"Then he would never conduct any type of marriage service if there were questions. Gean made it very clear to him when asked what her intentions were."

"What did she say, Leroy?" the sheriff asked.

"To be married to Bo Hackney."

"Liar! Ambrose turned to the sheriff. "He's lying!"

"Ambrose, I'll check with the pastor but if this is true there isn't anything I can do. Gean is a grown woman."

"He forced her! My Gean would never marry that trash!"

Leroy placed his cup on the rail, walking down the stairs to where Ambrose stood.

"I told you six years ago, Bo is not trash. Gean is an intelligent woman who is capable of making her own decisions. It appears you weren't able to control every facet of her life like you do Lillie's."

"Leroy!" the sheriff said.

Ambrose broke away from the sheriff hitting Leroy in the face. "Mind your business! What I do in my home is not your concern! Bo Hackney forced my daughter to marry him and you helped!"

The sheriff intervened again pulling him back. "That's enough, Ambrose. Are you okay, Leroy?"

Wiping the blood from his mouth he nodded. "I'm fine."

"Do you know where they went?" the sheriff asked.

Leroy shook his head no. "They left an hour after the ceremony. Neither of them said where they were headed or for how long. Out of respect for the newlyweds, I didn't ask."

Ambrose paced back and forth stopping to point his finger at Leroy. "This isn't over! I'll find them and have the marriage annulled. Gean deserves better, I'll see she gets better!"

"It appears to me Ambrose, she married the best."

Ambrose swung out again at Leroy. The sheriff pushed him away. "Leave Ambrose! Or I'll put you in jail."

They watched as he drove away leaving a large dust trail behind him.

"I'm sorry, Leroy. When he said Gean had been kidnapped I didn't have a choice."

"I expected as much, sheriff. Everybody in town knows Gean and Bo were in love. The only person who didn't see it was Ambrose."

"You shouldn't have said anything about Lillie."

Leroy kicked the dirt at his feet and nodded. "I don't approve of how he treats his wife."

"It isn't your business even though I know how you feel about her. Why didn't you marry her all those years ago?"

"I couldn't give her the things Ambrose offered. The early years out on the ranch were difficult. It's not proper to ask a woman to live under the stars, no place to wash up but the creek."

The sheriff nodded. "I don't believe I've ever seen him this upset. Bo and Gean need to stay gone for a while, let him come to terms with their marriage."

"Sheriff, I thought you knew Ambrose. He may never come to terms with this situation. I hope Lillie will be able to calm him down and talk some sense into him."

"I hope you're right. Ambrose is not a man to be trifled with as you well know. I don't want to hear Bo has disappeared one day."

"I'm pretty sure Gean will never allow anything to happen to Bo."

"If you hear from them I'd appreciate a call."

Leroy began to laugh. "Sheriff, I think they will have better things to do than calling me."

"You know, I'm happy for them and wish the best."

Leroy placed his hand on the sheriff's shoulder. "They will be just fine, sheriff. I expect them to do well together, you'll see. How about a cup of coffee and I'll show you the new house."

"Sounds good to me."

Ambrose drove the now dust-covered Cadillac back to his home. He took the time to think and make a plan to find and bring Gean back. The longer she was gone the more damage could be done. Once they were located Gean would be sent away for at least a year. He would send her up north from all the gossip of Glenmore.

The marriage would be annulled, if she was pregnant the baby would be adopted by a good family. Their child could never be connected to the Glenmore fortune. An offer of money would be made to Bo, any refusal meant a permanent removal from town. Stopping the car, he could see Lillie at the top of the steps. He slammed the car door, storming towards her like a bull, puffing with every breath.

"You didn't find them, did you?"

"Shut up woman! You know I didn't or she'd be with me. How could you just let her leave?"

"What in God's name did you expect me to do? By the time I discovered the letter she was gone."

"You could've called the sheriff."

"And told him what? My grown daughter has run away?"

He pushed past her to enter the house, slamming the screen door in Lillie's face.

"Damn you, Ambrose Glenmore!" She followed him inside. "You are going to hear me out for once. I don't care if you kill me."

Ambrose turned around raising his hand at the small woman who dared to challenge him.

"Go ahead. Hit me! I will have my say and you will listen for once in your miserable life."

Ambrose lowered his hand. "What do you have to say, woman?"

"You are responsible for all of this!"

"Leroy Grinder is..."

"No! You thought our daughter could be molded into a version of yourself. You failed! Continuing down this road will succeed in one thing."

"Gean will succeed where I failed. She will carry the Glenmore legacy into the future taking back everything owed to this family."

Lillie frowned shaking her head. "All this will do is force her to leave Glenmore with Bo, never to return."

"What do you know? Gean is..."

"A married woman who has slept with her husband. She is no longer the virgin you were going to place up for sale to the highest bidder."

"Stop! I swear if you don't stop."

"Do you possibly think the people in town don't know? Billie Dwyer, her best friend, and Millie from the restaurant have already called this morning. They want to know why Gean was married at the Circle G instead of the church. In the town's eyes, she is a tarnished woman or pregnant."

"Enough! I'll fix this. I can make it right!"

"Ambrose, our daughter is no longer a child. She is a grown woman who made a choice. Whether it is right or wrong it was hers to make. We cannot change it."

"He forced her! Bo and Leroy forced her!"

Lillie took a moment to look at her husband, almost feeling sorry for him. "You are the only fool in town who couldn't see the truth. Accept what has been done or lose her forever."

Chapter 8

Happy Life
    1962

Bo Hackney drove the 1962 Blue Chevy pickup to the hangar at the edge of his land. Turning off the motor, he leaned back into the seat and thought about the last twenty years of his life. Rubbing his head over the headache which started this morning. He would forever be in Leroy Grinder's debt for believing a runaway could become more than a charity case or criminal. The love of a young girl proved there were no boundaries in what two people could accomplish. They were very fortunate financially with several sound investments over the years.

His biggest disappointment was Ambrose's refusal to acknowledge their accomplishments and the treatment of Blessan. Bo hoped the birth of a grandchild would chisel away the hate and anger over their marriage, it didn't. She was a copy of Gean in her thoughtful and caring manner. As a child, there wasn't anything she wouldn't do if asked. He had tried to instill a sense of responsibility and pride in her work. Fierce and unforgiving anger to injustice or disloyalty to family was Blessan's only flaw. In his opinion, she had a propensity to overreact in these situations occasionally.

The last time he was in the Glenmore home was on Blessan's sixth birthday. Ambrose made a comment forcing him to finally take the man outside to have a conversation.

"I'll not upset the women with what I have to say."

"Out of my way trash," Ambrose said trying to push Bo aside.

He held the man up against the outside of the house. "I am not trash and you will not treat or speak to my daughter as you did inside ever again, understood?

"I said nothing."

"Criticizing her for being a girl is the wrong thing to do. Blessan will be given every opportunity to be the individual she chooses. I can accept your anger and hatred but she is a child and does not understand. Your actions as a grandfather are hurtful. Ambrose, you are a despicable human being."

Though Gean and Blessan returned occasionally when Ambrose was away on business, he never went back. He opened the truck door sliding out, reaching in the back for a large black leather bag. Arriving at the hangar he dropped the bag and opened the metal door. The squeak and moan of the door increased the pounding in his head. It ceased momentarily when he caught sight of the Cessna 150. Bo loved this plane never regretted the purchase, despite the continuing criticism from his father-in-law to anyone who would listen. The sound of a car horn forced him to step out seeing Gean's red 1960 Mustang. Walking up to the car he frowned discovering she was alone.

"Why the ugly face?" she asked.

"Where's Blessan?"

Gean began to laugh. "I left her and Leroy arguing over who is a better ranch foreman, men or women."

Bo held his hands up backing away. "Lord, I am extremely happy not to be a part of that conversation. I need some help moving the plane out."

"Are you ready to go?" Gean asked.

"Almost, I still need to do a preflight check. I thought Blessan wanted to go with us." Bo said.

"She changed her mind when Leroy said there were cattle missing and fences to repair," Gean answered.

They moved the plane outside for Bo to begin his preflight check. He stopped rubbing his head.

"Gean, can you run into the hangar and find the aspirin?"

She walked away returning with a cup of water and a small bottle. "Headache from the party?"

"You have to admit Amos threw a celebration. I think the entire town was there," he said taking the water and bottle. Pouring out two tablets he took them.

"Your hangover might not have been so bad if you had taken time to eat," she said.

"Amos was so proud of Billie and the new building. How could I say no to free whiskey? I did eat, just not enough."

"I hope they didn't waste any leftover food. It would be a nice treat for the residents at the nursing home," she said.

"Hopefully Billie will allow Amos to take it to them."

"I never expected the two of them to stay around after passing the state bar. Billie always wanted to live the big city life in Austin or San Antonio," she said.

"There probably isn't a large calling for farm equipment in either of those cities."

"I agree. Amos would never sell his family business no matter how much money Billie would make as an attorney."

"I was surprised when he bought the building," he said.

"The office is a peace offering for refusing to move away. She seemed happy last night. Bo, why was Ivan McMinn there?"

He began to laugh. "The town bookie? I'm sure he was there to either pay Amos or collect."

"His gambling is going to be an issue one day," she said.

His check complete, he stood for a moment staring at the plane.

"I don't guess we could postpone this trip?" he asked attempting to look sad.

"Nice try but a self-induced hangover doesn't override a contract with the Santa Fe railroad. Time to saddle up."

I didn't think so but it was worth a try."

She reached out taking his arm. "We've been married long enough for me to know when something is bothering you. What is it?"

"Do you think Blessan is happy?"

"You need to be a little more specific here."

"Is she happy living and working on a ranch instead of going to college and doing something else with her life?"

"You mean like being a secretary or nurse instead of riding horses and chasing cows?"

"I wanted a better life for her. Be a lady and wear a dress if she had one."

"Bo Hackney, your daughter is a lady who owns several dresses. She happens to prefer boots and jeans. Blessan has always been strong-willed even as a child. If she prefers to ride a horse or work the ranch over sitting in an office typing, then good for her."

He began laughing. "She reminds me of someone else." Raising his head to the sky and pointing at the dark clouds. "We need to go before these get any worse."

"I agree, though they're not in the direction we are headed," she said. Gean pointed back towards the leather bag. "Please don't forget that."

Walking away to grab the bag. "You know how fast the weather can change here. Did you mail your package?" he asked.

"No. I gave it to Billie last night. She promised to mail it today."

Bo opened the door of the plane and entered. "I'm not sure this project of yours is such a good idea, it could hurt or embarrass a lot of people."

She smiled. "You worry too much; besides I can cancel the contract at any time."

"If I have a vote in this, canceling is the best option."

Gean closed the door to the Cessna. Bo taxied the plane out on to the dirt runway.

"I'll think about it," she said.

Chapter 9

Black Tears

One-week later Glenmore Cemetery

The skies were dark and clouds hung over the cemetery with a constant threat to the people below. The weather did not keep the citizens of Glenmore from paying their respects to Blessan and the Glenmore family. The successful trip to Houston turned deadly. The small Cessna was not equipped to handle the sudden change of weather on Bo and Gean's return home. The Walsh's stood outside the tent several rows back from the gravesite. Every business in town closed itsdoors to show respect.

Moving slightly to one side Billie glanced around the couple in front of them to see Leroy Grinder standing behind Blessan. Lillie Glenmore sat alone next to her granddaughter leaving the question everyone there wanted to know. Where was Ambrose? It was no secret how he felt about Bo, but how could anyone not support your own flesh and blood? As the pastor said his final words over the caskets of Gean and Bo Hackney a light rain began to fall.

Billie raised her eyes to the sky. "Jesus Christ, could it not have waited until we were in the car to do this? I hate funerals!"

"Damn it, Billie! Gean was your best friend. Show some respect," Amos scolded.

"I can show respect in the car," she said leaning into Amos. "I heard the railroad accepted Gean's contract. Look at her Amos. Blessan Hackney has just become one of the wealthiest women in Texas. I bet in a month she leaves this little shithole town to move south."

Looking at his wife scowling. "Is money all you can think of? I doubt she gives a damn how much is in a bank account."

"Don't be naive. Money, especially the kind she will inherit can ease a lot of pain and grief. I can only dream of what would be possible with her fortune," she said.

He shook his head. "You are unbelievable."

Billie noticed a shift in the crowd and could see Ivan moving towards them. He stopped next to Amos offering a simple handshake completing their transaction.

"I hope that was to your benefit," she said sarcastically.

"It certainly was," Amos smiled.

"Good. I'm certainly tired of being on the short end of your bad habits," Billie said.

"My bad habits make your shopping trips to Dallas for the last two years possible."

The crowd began to move towards Blessan and Lillie. Billie walked away to stand under a tree, Amos following her.

"Why'd you come over here?" Amos asked.

"I want to wait until the crowd has moved away from them."

They stood for a few moments. The wind direction changed bringing with it the stench of the local feed yard. Billie took her gloved hand and covered her nose.

"Smells like money," Amos said.

"Smells like rancid cow shit," she said.

"Let's make our way up to Blessan. The crowd is beginning to thin out," he said.

The flash of lightning and a crash of thunder caused the skies to open. The light rain turned into a downpour.

"God, I hate the weather and this town! You make our condolences. I'm going to the car."

Billie took the only umbrella they brought leaving Amos to walk in the downpour. She hurried to the car cursing with each wet step she took. A few moments later Amos opened the door. The gust of wind and rain-soaked the cloth seat. He closed a small umbrella.

"Where did you get that?" she asked

"Ivan had an extra one with him."

"I can't believe he didn't charge you for it. Let's go home," she said.

He started the car and began to drive out of the cemetery with the rest of the mourners.

"Ivan told me Ambrose didn't come to the funeral because he is sick," Amos said.

"Sick with a cold?" she asked.

"No. Sick as in cancer. Rumor is, he's dying."

"We all die, Amos, some sooner than others. I bet Lillie leaves here once he's gone. I heard he was a violent old son-of-a-bitch to her," she said.

"There's no proof of that," Amos said.

"How could there be proof? Women weren't allowed to complain about the abuse they received years ago. He was a bastard then and still is," she said.

"Ivan said it's some type of lung cancer."

"He's been a smoker as long as I can remember. Gean would pick cigarettes up for him at the feed store years ago. She used it as an excuse to meet Bo when Flo and I weren't available to cover for her."

"It's a bad way to go."

"I didn't know there was a good way to die," she said.

"Billie, what's in the package on the dining room table?"

"I don't know. Gean gave it to me the night of the party to mail for her," she answered.

"Why didn't you?"

"I intended to mail it. When we received word they had been killed it didn't seem important at the time."

"I'll take it to Blessan tomorrow," he said.

"Amos, let's wait on returning it."

"Why?"

"If Gean wanted Blessan to have it why didn't she give it to her?"

"Billie you can't keep it! Whatever is in the package belongs to Blessan, return it!"

"I'm not going to discuss this with you right now. Gean asked me to take care of it for her. I intend to honor that last request."

Billie listened to the wipers and watched as the rain increased in intensity. She began to think about the package. Why would Gean not ask her daughter to mail it? Blessan would need time to heal after the death of her parents. There wasn't a need to return it or mail it. She would keep it for now. It was for the best.

II

Time Forward

Chapter 10

1969

Leroy Grinder drank hot black coffee in the library of his home. He attempted to understand the bad things people do to one another in the name of fame and money. At seventy he was happy to still have all his teeth and most of his hair. Admitting his eyes were no longer the deep blue they once were but hard work changes you eventually. The younger man full of spit and fire received two broken ribs from a young calf during branding this year, setting him back a few months. His foreman came one day asking, no actually begging him to take things a little slower. His ranch hands were more than capable of doing the harder work. They would like to keep him around for a few more years.

The Circle G had been an active part of the community for over forty years, helping the city and neighbors when called upon. He sent word for his foreman to come to the house for a meeting. His recent discovery of theft and betrayal would not be a pleasant conversation to have, but necessary.

The sound of the old ranch pickup caused him to move towards the large window where a large dust trail formed. His white starched shirt and denim jeans had their first crease of the day. The ranch foreman's performance over the last two years was outstanding. There were turbulent times at the beginning among the cowboys. A few thought they were more capable of doing the job and spoke up.

"Guadalupe!"

A small Hispanic woman entered the library. Wiping her hands on the red-striped apron.

"Yes, Mr. Leroy."

"Would you please bring more coffee and your special donuts to the library?"

She left the room. The front door opened followed by the sound of boots, spurs, and the patter of paws coming down the wood hallway.

"You needed to see me, sir?"

"Come in Blessan. We need to talk," Leroy told her.

The young woman entered the library with a large German Shephard by her side.

"Shephard sit," Blessan ordered.

Leroy walked over and rubbed the dog's head pulling a treat from his jean pocket giving it to the dog.

"You spoil him," she said.

"He deserves it."

Blessan found Shephard in a box by the front gate of the ranch. Animals were frequently discarded in the country by uncaring owners and his property had not been immune. This puppy was fortunate, as most were met with untimely deaths due to vehicles or predators. Shephard's arrival came at a much-needed time in Blessan's' life. He became a companion and as she said best buddy.

"Good morning, Guadalupe," Blessan said. Removing her duster then following the housekeeper to the small buffet.

"Good morning, Miss Blessan."

Guadalupe reached down and gave the dog a treat. She rubbed his head and said something in Spanish which made him lick the woman's hand.

Blessan shook her head. "He's going to get fat."

"He keeps the coyotes away from my chickens. He needs his strength," Guadalupe told her.

Leroy laughed.

"Donuts? This must be important," Blessan said.

"Any issues with the men?"

Blessan laughed. "You mean other than the usual?"

"You are the youngest of the group. I figured there would be some problems."

"I know twenty-seven is young, but I shoot better, and can outdrink all of them except old Ralph. I work hard every day as they do."

"I've been told you seem to have a special ability to find the strays."

"I don't know about it being special. I just seem to know where they like to hide. I understand it's difficult to take orders from a woman. I have offset their reluctance, with respect and praise when it is deserved."

"And?"

"The slackers can find another place to work, it's that simple."

"I was given some grief over promoting you."

"Oh, I'm sure you were."

"Blessan, you have proven a woman is capable of doing this job. I made the right decision."

"Thank you. Dad would tell me, as a small girl, to always work hard and do my best."

"Your father was like a son to me."

Blessan began to smile. "Dad didn't speak too much of his life before coming to the Circle G. I respected his decision to consider the Circle G home and you family. A foreman on any job will have conflict at times. I've learned to deal with the accusations of favoritism and ignore the comments. It works best not to engage or lower myself."

"I intended to pass this ranch on to Bo one day. He worked hard in the early years. No one deserved it more than he did."

"I miss them terribly."

"We all do, Blessan."

"You know Dad swore me to secrecy."

"About what exactly?"

"Your part in their courtship and marriage."

Leroy thought back to the day Gean took a seat on the tailgate of his old pickup. "I have never seen two people who were meant to be together like your folks."

"I agree."

"Your grandfather planned Gean's future which didn't include Bo."

"I think he intended to send mom out east to college. Once she received a degree, he planned to marry her off to the highest bidder."

Leroy gave Blessan a stern look.

"Ambrose intended to build an alliance among strong landholders south of Glenmore, increase his wealth and power through marriage. There were several wealthy men north and south of Glenmore with eligible sons. Gean would not had any say in who she married. He never counted on his daughter falling in love with Bo."

"I don't think Papa counted on you intervening," she said.

"Have you heard from your grandmother?"

Blessan smiled. "She's doing well in her little condo in St. Augustine. Florida has been good for her."

"I have to say she surprised everyone here in town."

"Blessan laughed. Grandmother told me when Papa became ill she would not stay here once he passed. I can't blame her for moving so far away from Glenmore. She's a very wealthy widow."

"Maybe, I'll go visit one day," Leroy smiled.

"I think she would like to see you. Grandmother never spoke of her younger years when Papa was alive. We had several conversations over glasses of Wild Turkey once he was gone."

"Lillie is a beautiful woman."

Blessan smiled.

Leroy walked over to the wall safe, opened it, and took out a package.

"I have a good friend in San Antonio who is an attorney. He sent this to me a few weeks ago, thought I might be interested in the contents."

He handed the package to her. She moved to a chair opening the box. He could see her hands shaking once the item was removed. Blessan opened the book looking through several pages.

"I always wondered what happened to mothers manuscript." She leaned back into the chair, eating a second donut and sipping on coffee. "Did he say who sent this to him?"

"He advised it came from an associate of ours."

"Boss, this isn't just concerning. It is a major problem for everyone in the city."

"Agreed."

"Are there any options, or recourse?" she asked.

"I spoke with him at length, asking the same questions. He said any direct legal actions would be time-consuming, and expensive with little hope of a positive outcome. The best option at this point would be a delay."

Shaking her head. "I wasn't expecting this to be the reason for donuts today."

"I've been conflicted over involving you in this issue since I received it."

Blessan stood up walking over to the window. Shephard sensing the tension moved quickly to her side, nudging a hand. Reaching down touching him encouraged the dog to lean against her leg.

"Boss, you should have told me sooner. This is not something you need to handle alone."

"You've had enough to deal with since the accident," he said.

"I have unfortunately discovered since their death certain individuals are not trustworthy. It's one of the reasons I moved out here. To stop any gossip on my inheritance, I split it between the banks in Houston, Dallas, and El Paso."

"The majority of citizens in Glenmore are good honest people."

She smiled. "I know, it's one of the reasons I have to help you."

Leroy walked over and stood next to her.

"Blessan, I'd appreciate any suggestions you might have to help me with this problem."

Blessan stood for a few moments, then turned to face him.

"I know that look on your face. What are you thinking?" he smiled.

"Boss, do you still have friends in New York?"

"I do."

Chapter 11

Easy Money
  1972

Billie Walsh walked towards the exit of the county courthouse quite pleased with the outcome of the morning's hearing. She never went unnoticed due to the click of heels on the marble floor and heavy breathing that echoed in the hallway. Being assigned the administrator over another Will where no executor was named added money to the office account. She was an expert at discovering these situations over the years.

Her secretary would file the necessary paperwork with the clerk. Outstanding bills would be paid and she would happily charge inflated fees from the office to the county for payment. In all of these cases, there would be little or no money left for the court to distribute. In a few she managed to show her office lost money, at least on paper.

"Got another one did you, Wilhelmina?" a deep male voice asked.

"Jackson, you know these things never pay well."

Laughing loudly walking towards her. "In most cases, that statement would be true, though I've never known you to work for free."

She stopped, turning around and looking up. "Jackson, you know after all these years I despise being called by my given name."

He smiled. "I heard you were at the nursing home looking for victims last week."

Billie's face turned red feeling the anger rising.

"I have business waiting for me at the office. Tell Florence I said hello."

"You might want to make an appointment with her, your grey is showing. Oh, Happy Birthday, fifty-two isn't it?"

She didn't respond, turning and hurrying out the door. Bantering with the biggest gossip in town was useless even though he was an associate. Billie had been correct all those years ago knowing Jackson Hellman would make something of himself. The disappointment came when he married Flo and remained in Glenmore. He was tall, with thick wavy hair with the slightest grey beginning to appear on the sides. His round wire-rimmed glasses gave him a scholarly appearance, with those deep hazel eyes.

He was quite the charmer in his early days. She would never forgive Florence Bigalow for leaving with Jackson that afternoon. If she hadn't been covering for Bo and Gean one summer afternoon and gone to Amarillo things might have been different today. Her last name might be Hellman instead of Walsh.

She missed her chance with Bo, too. Billie tried flirting with him while Gean was away at boarding school. He politely explained they could be friends, nothing more. This left overweight, Amos Walsh. The incentive to become involved with him was due to the eventual inheritance of the family business. Promising to shower her with money, cars, and pay for college all sealed the deal on his marriage proposal.

Shaking her head realizing marriage to Jackson might have been worse than being married to Amos. Entering the Range Rover, she looked in the rearview mirror towards the courthouse.

"He is such an ass sometimes."

Driving two blocks to a small building she noticed the morning sun disappearing behind rapidly forming dark clouds. In the Texas panhandle, this wasn't an unusual occurrence but it did cause folks to watch the skies for tornados. Many could form and touch down before the sirens could alert anyone to seek shelter. Opening the glass door to a buzzer that announced her arrival. The older woman at the reception desk smiled.

"Good morning, Billie. I hear we're going to have a storm later."

"Good morning, Penny. I believe it's early. Please make me an appointment with Flo for a cut and color this week."

"I'll do it right now," Penny answered.

Billie turned back to the door as lightning flashed across the dark cloud, followed by a crackling sound of thunder.

"I hate this type of weather."

"How did things go this morning in court?"

Billie made a thumbs-up sign heading towards her office.

"You have an appointment at three with Blessan Hackney."

Billie stopped, turning around. "Good Lord, Gean and Bo's daughter."

"Yes."

"I haven't spoken to Blessan since her parents' funeral."

"They've been gone ten years this month. A small plane crash wasn't it?" Penny asked.

"Yes. A storm very similar to this one. One reason I won't fly in those little death traps." Billie shivered.

"I know what you mean."

"Did Blessan say why she was coming in?"

"No. I remember the funeral too. She looks so much like her mother."

"Blessan is tall, slender like Bo, but has Gean's chestnut hair and green eyes."

"Gean was a Glenmore, wasn't she?" Penny asked.

"Yes. Her family owned all the land this town is built on. They made a lot of money farming and raising cattle."

"The oil they found didn't hurt either," Penny said.

Billie smiled. "No, it didn't.

"I always thought the way Gean spelled her name was a terrible mistake," Penny said.

"Oh, it was no mistake. Gean's father is the one who chose the spelling of her name."

"Why would Mr. Glenmore do such a thing to his daughter?" Penny asked.

"He was a ruthless old bastard in his day. One of the rumors I was told said he had her name spelled differently to ensure success in a man's world. She would never have a chance to prove it as a Glenmore but did as a Hackney. Gean took advantage of the way her name was spelled. It allowed loans and deals that would not have been possible if the other parties knew she was a woman."

"I heard Gean's father didn't like Bo."

"Bo worked for Leroy Grinder as a ranch hand. He was not the type of man Ambrose wanted to see their debutant daughter marry. Her father made every decision from the clothes she wore to the fancy schools up east. He would never have given her permission to marry Bo. Gean was being groomed to marry someone who would increase the Glenmore dynasty."

"I have heard rumors over at Lynn's from the older folks Lillie never came to town much," Penny said.

"Lillie wasn't allowed to have an opinion on anything according to Gean. She was rarely seen in town. It wouldn't surprise anyone if he beat her," Billie said.

"Oh, how terrible. Was there any proof?"

"No, but you have to remember women had little or no rights back then especially here. It wasn't heard of for a woman to make a complaint of abuse against her husband. He owned her like property."

"I heard Mr. Glenmore's attorneys were ready to have Bo and Gean's marriage annulled," Penny said.

"I believe he would have forced Gean into an annulment if they had been found. Ambrose blamed Leroy for their elopement and went out to the Circle G himself to confront him."

"What do you mean by confronting him?"

"Old man Glenmore filed a kidnapping report on Bo. He took the sheriff out to the Circle G claiming he was complicit in forcing the marriage. Gean was grown and there was nothing the sheriff could do."

"I hadn't heard this story. She didn't tell you or Flo about her plans?"

"Flo and I would help Gean sneak out to be with Bo when she was home for the summers and school breaks. I thought she would have said something about their plans since we were best friends. The only person who knew was Leroy. I understand he drove to the preacher's house, woke him up, and barely allowed the man to dress. Leroy then drove them to the Circle G giving no explanation until they arrived."

"What about her mother?" Penny asked.

"Years later Lillie told Flo at the shop, she went out early to feed chickens. When Gean didn't come down for breakfast she went to check on her. Lillie found a letter explaining they eloped."

"I bet it didn't take long for the word to spread through the town."

Billie smiled. "They were gone for three weeks after the ceremony. Ambrose hired a couple of men to search for them. He was determined to bring her back, save her reputation, and move forward with his plans."

"Did they find them?"

"No. When they returned Ambrose drove out to their home. I'm not privy to their entire conversation. Gean told Ambrose it was her who was pushing the pregnancy rumors all over town."

"Were there rumors?" Penny asked.

"Of course. The old women in town blew up the phone lines. A decent woman just didn't run off and get married outside the church. Unless you were tarnished or pregnant." Billie laughed.

"He couldn't force an annulment."

"No, the damage so to speak was done. A defiant daughter, married to a nobody and pregnant."

Penny laughed. "I guess Blessan's birth two years later disappointed a few people."

"You might say that Ambrose was disappointed when Blessan was born never treating her the way a grandfather should. His wife failed him by not producing a male heir and now Gean failed too. He made comments in town saying Bo came from bad breeding stock."

"What a terrible thing to say?"

"Yes, it was," Billie answered.

"How could you treat your grandchild in such a manner?" Penny asked.

"I heard Blessan spent a week helping Lillie take care of Ambrose out at the Glenmore home. She sat at his bedside holding his hand until passed. The old bastard never once spoke her name."

"Goodness," Penny said shaking her head.

"I did hear a few years before he stopped coming into town Ambrose finally admitted he'd been wrong to judge Bo so harshly. It appeared his son-in-law had a head for business, despite the lack of a college degree."

"Did he say it to Bo?"

"No," Billie answered.

"I bet Leroy Grinder had something to do with Bo's ability to make good investments."

Billie nodded. "Leroy raised Bo."

"Bo and Gean seemed to have done well over the years they were married."

"Yes, they did. He made several investments with large returns. The railroad contract signed before they died added to the huge inheritance for their only child."

"I was surprised when she called. Is she still out at Grinder's?" Penny asked.

Billie shook her head and began to laugh. "According to Jackson, she is the foreman out there."

"How would he know?" Penny asked.

"Jackson is not only the court gossip, he knows everything of importance within a hundred miles of town. I've seen the two of them at Lynn's coffee shop several times over the years."

"Guess it's true then," Penny laughed.

"She is unimaginably wealthy with endless choices. Blessan could live anywhere, even in another country, and be treated like royalty. Instead, she's running cattle, living in a bunkhouse full of rowdy cowboys and choosing to work every day except Sunday."

"She's about twenty-eight isn't she?"

"No. I believe she's thirty."

"Billie, can I get you some coffee?"

She nodded. "I'll be in the office."

Billie dropped the leather briefcase on a large desk. Removing a file as Penny entered with a large arrangement of pink roses and coffee.

"Happy Birthday."

"Penny these weren't necessary, thank you. I need this processed as usual." Billie handed the file from the court.

"Right away. Flo called back. She's double-booked for Saturday and asked if you would come in early?"

"What time?"

"She said to be there at eight or you'll have to wait another week."

"I'd wait another week, but Jackson made a remark on my grey hair. Call her back and tell her I'll be there."

"Anything else, Billie?"

"No."

She took a moment admiring the arrangement. Penny was a wonderful employee working with her since the office doors opened. She has a propensity for town gossip causing issues at times for the office. Although there were problems occasionally some information was extremely helpful on a few of Billie's cases.

She turned as the rain began hitting heavily on the window obscuring one of the two traffic signals in town. Stepping back against the desk with the realization as to the possibility of today's meeting with Blessan. Bo and Gean must have left their child's inheritance in a trust. Why would she have worked all these years for Leroy Grinder with all that money? She was practically hyperventilating at the thought of handling such a large fortune. Walking quickly out to Penny's desk.

"Do you know if Blessan ever received her inheritance?"

"I can't say for positive."

"Is Jo Beth Martin still working at the bank?"

"Yes. I'll give her a quick call. If anyone will know it's Jo Beth," Penny answered.

Billie walked back to her desk and began to quickly formulate a plan. She would estimate her fees on the high end for all services. The timing was perfect with the anniversary of Bo and Gean's accident. She had a special tactic for clients in times of sorrow or uncertainty. Moving from behind the desk sitting close taking their hands and waiting for the perfect moment to smile. Softly and with the sincerest voice possible her speech began to the grief-stricken.

"I'll be pleased to help you, this is why I became an attorney. In situations like these, it's for the best."

Chapter 12

Unfortunate News

Blessan disliked the hard downpours of the Texas spring storms but knew they would pass, sometimes as quickly as they came. The wipers on the truck no longer kept up with the rain causing her to slow down to keep in the proper lane of traffic. Parking on the street in front of Wilhelmina Walsh's office she buttoned the duster. The collar turned up and the baseball cap pulled down tight. She turned to look at Shepard sitting next to the passenger door.

"You stay put. This shouldn't take long."

The dog whined lying down on the bench seat. She hurried to the front door of the office. The wind first blew the door open then it shut hard causing the glass to rattle. She took a breath, thankful it hadn't shattered. When she turned around an older woman stood smiling at her.

"I'm so sorry, I couldn't catch the door," Blessan said, removing her cap and duster.

"Quite the storm. I'll take those, can I get you something to drink?" Penny said.

Blessan hesitated a moment before handing the wet items to her.

"No, nothing to drink, thank you. I have an appointment with Mrs. Walsh."

"I'm Penny, her assistant. She's expecting you."

Blessan walked over to the office and stopped before knocking on the doorframe. The woman behind the desk smiled, motioning her to enter. Mrs. Walsh hadn't changed in the past ten years. Still the same small overweight woman with an outdated hairstyle and poor choice in apparel. The Walsh's were her parents' good friends at one time. Amos passed away the year after her parents.

"Blessan Hackney, it's been forever since I've seen you. Come in, please sit down. Did Penny offer you something to drink?"

"Yes, she did, thank you, Mrs. Walsh."

"Billie, please call me Billie. What can I do for you today?"

Blessan sat down in the uncomfortable straight-back chair. The one reason for such types of furniture was to keep unwanted clients out and force the good ones to hurry with business.

"Mr. Grinder asked me to come in and speak to you."

"Leroy? What is that old cowboy up to these days?"

"He's up in years as you know, seventy-three. It's been some time since he's been able to actively work the ranch. He has begun to have health issues."

"I would imagine you handle all the work out there for him. I hear you're the foreman."

"Yes, ma'am. He doesn't have any family..."

"No family? I thought he had a sister?"

"He does, did," Blessan answered.

"I'm sorry to hear that. Did she have children?"

"I can't say for sure, he has never mentioned anyone."

"What was his sister's name, it seems to have slipped my memory?"

"Bernadette."

"That's right, she ran off to California. The last thing I heard she was entering a convent."

Blessan knew where this conversation was headed.

"Mrs. Walsh."

"My apologies. What can I do for you today?" Billie asked.

"Mr. Grinder has offered to sell the ranch to me. He is requesting your services to have papers drawn for the sale."

Billie leaned back in her chair. "This is a pleasant surprise. I thought Jackson would have been his choice. I know they are close friends."

"Mr. Grinder felt your experience in dealing with this type of situation would be handled quietly. He needs this done quickly."

"Did you say Leroy is having health issues?"

"He has been diagnosed with cancer."

Billie leaned forward entwining her hands. "The Circle G has been such a viable part of our community over the years. This is very sad to hear."

"I intend for it to remain a viable asset to the town," Blessan said.

"Oh, of course. Where is Leroy?"

"His physician referred him to Houston for treatments. He's been there a week. We would like to complete the sale quickly."

"Blessan, in situations like these, it's for the best. The Circle G could not be in more capable hands. I'll be happy to see a smooth transition."

"He has asked for you to come out to the ranch."

"Why? I will be able to obtain the information I need from the clerk's office."

"Mr. Grinder's illness is not public knowledge. He would appreciate all discretion in regards to his condition and the sale of the ranch."

"I understand."

Blessan watched as Billie opened a large folder, looking through several pages.

"Give me a minute, I haven't had a chance to check my schedule since Penny updated it for me this morning," Billie told her.

"I'm in no hurry."

"Tomorrow I will be in court most of the day. Would Friday be acceptable?" she asked Blessan.

"I'll make arrangements to have the information and updated maps of the property for you. If you feel the need to check property lines, I suggest you bring clothing appropriate for riding. Could you arrive by nine?"

"I do not see a problem, but I won't need to check property lines. I can't remember the last time I was on a horse."

"I will see you Friday." Blessan began to stand.

"Blessan, I do have a question," Billie said.

"About the ranch?"

"No. It's a personal question. I hope you don't mind?"

"It depends on the question," Blessan smiled.

"I thought once receiving your inheritance you'd move to a big city like

Dallas or Austin. A lovely woman with the build and beauty of a model would prefer a different lifestyle. Why are you still in this small town working on a ranch?"

Blessan blushed. "Thank you for the compliment. My heart and memories are here. Working at the ranch makes me happy."

"What about your parents' place?"

"I, I..."

"I didn't mean to make you uncomfortable. If I had your fortune I'd be gone."

Blessan didn't respond to her statement. She stood up, walking out into the main area of the building. Accepting the duster and cap from Penny, turning to look out the glass door at the dark skies. The downpour ceased and the winds had calmed for the moment.

She turned to Billie. "I don't believe you'll have any difficulty with the roads unless it continues to storm."

"I have four-wheel drive," Billie said.

"Good, I'll see you Friday morning at nine," Blessan said.

Billie and Penny stood in the window watching the old pickup drive away.

"Jo Beth is out today, one of her children is home ill. Was this about her inheritance?" Penny asked.

"No, actually it's something bigger."

Chapter 13

The Find

Billie felt invigorated as she left the office and began the trip out to the Circle G ranch Friday morning. She would have preferred an extra day of searching the clerk's records but Leroy's files would be needed for comparison. The knowledge Leroy Grinder has no living relatives, designated executor, or any individual with a power of attorney was ideal. This situation was a dream come true and she could not believe how it had fallen into her hands. This opportunity would pay for the financial debt Amos left when he died and push an older project forward out of the dark.

Amos's bad family genetics, overindulgence in liquor and cigars, led to a massive heart attack. His decision to buy a building instead of life insurance left her in a financial disaster. She was paying for their expensive home, office building, and a bank loan for her education. Amos wasn't even cold in the ground when Ivan McMinn showed up at the door with a gambling marker for over twenty thousand dollars. The past nine years were more than difficult and she was close to bankruptcy.

Praying the road to the main house at the ranch was better identified than the last trip several years ago. Imagining the overgrown brush hiding the main gate and muddy road facing her. An official road sign appeared indicating the Circle G ranch was two miles ahead. Billie pulled to the side of the road short of a huge locked gate with the Circle G brand on it. The brick walls on both sides were impressive. Leaning back in the leather seat, it appeared Leroy Grinder was doing better than she remembered.

The locked gate presented a problem with no call box available. A man appeared as if on cue riding a horse. He unlocked the gate allowing passage. Billie waved at the man as she drove over the cattle guard onto an unexpected asphalt road. Arriving at the house another surprise met her in the form of a paved circle drive. These improvements were more than interesting for an old cowboy like Leroy.

Exiting the Rover, taking a few moments to view the flat desolate land in every direction which surrounded the house. Why would an extremely rich, lovely young woman want to live out here was beyond any sane reasoning. Adjusting the tight skirt after ringing the bell she was surprised when an older Hispanic woman opened the door.

"May I help you?"

Billie was perturbed the woman was uninformed of this morning's appointment.

"Attorney Wilhelmina Walsh to see Blessan Hackney. I am expected."

The woman acknowledged, allowing her to enter.

"Please follow me."

Entering a small dining room off the kitchen where a set of yellow cups and plates sat on a matching tablecloth.

"Senora, the buffet is available for you, something to drink?"

"Decaf coffee with skim milk."

The situation was turning to disappointment as she hadn't expected to be served in the kitchen where the help ate. The formal dining room should have been prepared for an important meeting. Proceeding to the table she placed the briefcase on the floor. The small room was light, cheerful with the lingering smell of fresh paint.

The walls were accented with several paintings. Her first glance was the artwork, believing them to be cheap prints in poor quality frames. Walking up to the first painting on the east wall she gasped and stumbled backward. It was Georgia O'Keeffe and appeared to be original, not a print, this discovery made her hands shake. Leroy Grinder had something worth more than land or cattle. Moving to check each of the other paintings she made a note of the signatures on them. Returning to the O'Keeffe, Billie hoped neither Leroy nor

Blessan were intelligent enough to understand the significance of this piece or its worth.

"Good morning. Any issue with the roads?"

Billie jerked around to see Blessan and a huge dog in the doorway. "Goodness. You scared me to death. I didn't hear you."

She hoped Blessan hadn't seen her earlier reaction. Hesitating to move as the dog followed Blessan into the dining room.

"Any problems finding the ranch?" Blessan asked.

"No. It was a pleasant drive and the sign is new isn't it?"

"The county put it up a year ago. Grab your plate, I hope you're hungry. Guadalupe is a wonderful cook."

Billie didn't move.

Blessan turned around. "What's bothering you, Mrs. Walsh?"

"I'm not used to animals being in the house. He's quite large."

"Shephard go," Blessan said snapping her fingers. The dog turned and left the room.

Billie joined Blessan at the buffet.

"It looks delicious. I didn't know there was a housekeeper."

They filled their plates returning to the table taking seats across from one another.

"She has been with Mr. Grinder for over five years."

Guadalupe entered with a small pot of coffee for Billie and a glass of milk for Blessan. She took a small pitcher of milk placing it in front of Billie.

"My drive was filled with several surprises from the gate to the house."

"I assume you are speaking of the fresh coat of paint, new gate, and circle drive."

"I am very pleased to not be stepping in mud, the new road and drive are appreciated. I was pleased to not spend time searching for the entrance," Billie said.

"The gate was a necessity; we've had recent issues with trespassers. The road and circle drive was my doing. I was tired of all the mud, too."

"How did you know to send someone out to open the gate?"

"I was out this morning when you pulled up. I sent one of the men to let you in. I'm having a call box installed in a couple of weeks. The phone will ring to the house or bunkhouse."

"It appears you are bringing Leroy into the present. Blessan, I checked with the clerk's office and obtained their information on the ranch for comparison," Billie said.

"I believe you will find their files have not been updated in years. Everything you need is in the library except financial reports from out of town. They will be delayed a couple of days."

"Is there an issue?"

"A few years back Mr. Grinder began to invest his money in outside ventures. The banks need a few days to send my requests. I'll forward copies to your office."

"I thought he would have all this information in one location. It would certainly speed up the process for me."

Blessan laughed. "I agree with you. I encouraged him to hire a full-time secretary to keep his records and files in order. I am afraid my secretarial skills are lacking. I write the payroll checks when he is out of town. My knowledge of his personal business is limited."

"Blessan, our main focus should be on Leroy's health. I'll have plenty of time to go over his estate."

She stopped eating and bowed her head. "It's nice to know someone has plenty of time."

Billie took Blessan's hand. "What has happened?"

"I received a call this morning from his physician in Houston. The news is not good. We must proceed quickly."

Billie nodded then leaned back in her chair. "I'm going to indulge and have another biscuit; may I bring you one?"

"No. Thank you."

"Blessan, I noticed the paintings when I arrived. Do you know if these are the only ones in the house?"

"Mrs. Walsh..."

"Billie, please dear, call me Billie."

She returned to the table.

"Billie, there are paintings over the entire home, a glass cabinet with a bunch of old dusty books, and a gun collection in the library."

Billie moved her hands beneath the table twisting the napkin tightly.

"Are you aware of any appraisals or purchase vouchers?"

"You will need to speak to Mr. Grinder. The paintings have been here since I went to work for him. It's the same with the books."

Billie smiled. "I'll take a closer look, if they appear to be originals, I'll call in an appraiser."

"If it will speed the process of the sale please call the individuals who will be of most assistance to you."

She took Blessan's hand once again. "As I said in my office, in situations such as these I'm always happy to help, it's for the best."

"The library is prepared for you with reports over the last two years, updated maps of the property, and a mineral report from the government."

"Thank you, but actually, I'd prefer a tour of the home first. If it isn't too much trouble?"

"I'll have Guadalupe assist you. A foreman's job is outside mending fences and finding lost cattle."

"You go ahead."

"Billie, you should know Mr. Grinder has a safe in the library."

"Do you have access?"

"No. He assured me there wasn't anything of value in it. Will you be here when I return this evening?"

"No. I have an engagement in town."

Billie winced when Blessan whistled for Shephard. She followed them to the back door of the kitchen waiting until the old truck was out of view.

"Guadalupe!"

"Yes."

"I've been given unlimited access to the house. I will not need your assistance."

"As you wish, Mrs. Walsh."

Billie didn't waste a moment and took a small camera from her briefcase. She usually didn't need it, but today it will be invaluable. She began to photograph the paintings. The glass bookcase Blessan spoke of was an antique located in the hallway outside of the formal dining room.

"Guadalupe!"

"Yes, Mrs. Walsh."

"Where is the key to this?"

"Mr. Leroy has it."

"Is there an extra one here?"

"No."

"Are you sure Blessan doesn't have one?"

"Mr. Leroy is the only one."

"You may go."

Photographing the case from several angles then writing down names and titles of the books. She recognized Hemingway but was unfamiliar with Lewis Gaylord Clark or Bancroft. The last book on the bottom had an author name of either Hitter or Hiller.

Arriving in the library, she discovered the information Blessan said would be waiting. The painting on the wall behind the desk stopped her movement and she attempted not to scream. The piece staring back at her was a Renoir. She had seen this painting in a New York museum where it was on loan from a private collector. Opening the curtains slightly to photograph it so no flash would distort the picture. How the hell did Leroy get this painting?

Recovering from the shock of the Renoir she caught sight of the safe Blessan mentioned. It appeared to be good quality, combination plus two keys to open the door. She didn't believe for one moment Leroy didn't have something of value locked away.

Frowning at the "gun collection" on opposite sides of the door as you exited the library. She wasn't particularly impressed with old dusty guns but photographed them regardless. They may be of some worth to a collector.

Scanning the maps of the Circle G property noting Leroy increased his property by several hundred acres in the last two years. She folded them picking up the small box marked copies with her name on it. A large amount of information would require weeks of study and comparison with the clerk. Penny would be instructed to methodically check all the information as the sale contract was prepared. She was practically out of breath when returning to the kitchen.

"Guadalupe!"

"Yes, Mrs. Walsh."

"I am going to leave. Please tell Blessan I'll be in touch."

"May I get you something to drink before you leave?"

"Yes. A glass of champagne if you have it."

Leaving the ranch filled with champagne trying to visualize the job before her. Everything in the house needed to be authenticated including the Renoir and O'Keeffe. She would obtain a list of potential buyers allowing a small amount of information to leak out to the treasure found in this little corner of Texas. Christie's Auction House would be contacted for maximum exposure and top-selling prices on the important pieces.

Billie would allow Leroy Grinder to die before the sale of the ranch was finalized. As the attorney handling his estate at the time of death, she would continue to do so without question. Every item of value would be liquidated before the auction of the ranch. Blessan would be allowed to bid on the Circle G, along with other interested parties. There was a chance it might be more profitable to sell the ranch off in sections instead of one piece. This was an option to be considered, more buyers meant a bigger profit.

A huge payday arrived in the form of a simple mistake. She would no longer be the little town lawyer in deep serious debt. A better life was ahead at the expense of someone else.

Chapter 14

Lighting a Fire

Leroy was delighted to be back home, out on his property with Blessan and working alongside his men. The weeks in Houston had been grueling on him. He entered the small dining room where she waited to join him for lunch. Raising her head with a twisted mouth. This was a sign of frustration usually done shortly before a string of profanities escaped her lips. Handing several pieces of paper to him to view. He took a moment to study the contents and frowned throwing them on the table. Guadalupe entered the room with a plate of tamales followed by Shephard.

"Guadalupe, this looks good, but a cold beer will make mine better," he said.

"Miss Blessan?"

"Sweet tea, thank you."

Leroy waited a moment before speaking.

"How long has it been now, two months?"

"Closer to three. The bills began two days after she was here," Blessan said.

"Are we any closer to having paperwork ready to sign?"

"I doubt it."

"I know you've tried to call her."

"My finger is worn out dialing her number. She will not return my calls; however, she has been sending a constant parade of appraisers through here checking everything from the carpets to curtains while you were gone. I received a formal letter requesting access to the safe."

"You explained there was nothing of value or interest inside, correct?"

"Yes, sir."

"I'll take care of it. Guadalupe, please join us for lunch," Leroy called out.

She entered with a tray filled with bowls of beans, rice, and their drinks.

"It's good to have you back, Mister Leroy. Shephard and I missed you." Guadalupe gave the dog a warm tortilla.

"I think he put on weight while I was gone."

"I told you both to stop feeding him," Blessan scolded.

Leroy sat down as Guadalupe joined them. He began to reach for the bowl of rice when he noticed her beginning to pray. He stopped until she finished.

"I've never seen you pray here," he said.

"I pray for you all the time and Miss Blessan you just never see me," she said.

"Well thank you," he said.

"We all need to pray especially for that horrible woman," she said.

"What woman?" he asked.

"Billie," Blessan answered.

"Oh."

They ate lunch in silence except for Shephard chomping when Guadalupe snuck a tortilla to him. When they finished Blessan helped to clear the table.

"Thank you, Miss Blessan," Guadalupe said.

Leroy motioned for Blessan to follow him.

"Where's the dog?"

"I imagine with Guadalupe eating another warm tortilla," she said.

He closed the door to the library.

"I think it may be time for me to make a call. I know exactly what Billie Walsh is doing. Jackson and I have had enough discussions over the years in regards to her ambulance-chasing and inflated service prices."

Blessan laughed. "I never expected she would drag this out so long."

"Time is money to an attorney. She will delay this as long as possible. The diagnosis of cancer was the dinner bell ringing for her."

"Boss!"

Moving to his desk, he picked up the phone dialing Billie's office number.

He placed the phone on speaker motioning Blessan not to speak.

"Wilhelmina Walsh's office, Penny speaking. May we help you today?"

"Leroy Grinder here. I need to speak to Billie now!"

"Just a moment."

"She will never answer you," Blessan said.

"I'm counting on it," he said and winked.

"Mr. Grinder, Mrs. Walsh is not available, can I take a message?" Penny asked.

"Please notify Mrs. Walsh I will be there in thirty minutes. I expect her to return from where ever she is to meet me." Leroy disconnected.

"It's at least an hour," Blessan said.

"I know, but Billie doesn't have a clue where I am."

He stepped out of the library for a few minutes then returned.

"Instructions for Guadalupe?" she asked.

"The phone was ringing when I got to the kitchen," he said.

"I truly wish I could go with you."

"I will catch up with you later on her lack of progress. I do need your assistance before I leave."

"Whatever you need, boss."

Chapter 15

Pushing Buttons

Billie was reviewing the final appraisal report on the artwork and books. Her hands were shaking at the amount of money involved. The locked cabinet in the hallway held twenty books, five were possibly first editions. If the books were in good or in pristine condition the price could double. The voice of one appraiser began to tremble when Billie faxed a copy of the list and photographs. The Hiller book was Hitler, Adolph Hitlers', "Mein Kampf". If it was signed, as he did on a selected few, the price would increase substantially.

A gun collector from Wyoming contacted her practically speechless one afternoon.

"Mrs. Walsh, my name is Bill Hansen. I'm an antique gun collector known to my friends as Wild Bill. Your name was sent to me with information on a rare gun collection you may be acquiring soon."

"It's in an estate which I will be handling the liquidation of assets. The collection will be part of this."

"I would appreciate the opportunity to make an offer to keep them from going to auction," he said.

"Unfortunately the appraisals have not returned on them. I cannot accept any offer at this time," Billie told him.

"I can assure you, Mrs. Walsh, my offer will be fair."

"It is just not possible until I receive the paperwork from the appraiser."

His tone increased. "Mrs. Walsh, I implore you to consider an offer."

"Have a nice day, I will be in touch," she said hanging up the phone.

Billie misjudged the dusty old guns in the library. The response of the collector was interesting. She would notify him in a few weeks requesting his offer. It would need to be several thousand over appraisal price if he wished to be considered.

Disbelief among appraisers, collectors, and the art world in general over the location of such treasures in our little corner of the world. Many were appalled at the manner these items were being displayed. Interest and tension were building on a release date of the painting to Christieres. The individual she spoke with indicated there was great anticipation.

Billie's plan was progressing nicely. The paperwork and sale of the ranch was placed to the side for now. The collections inside the house were the immediate priority. Looking up as Penny ran into the office.

"Billie, Leroy Grinder called and he will be here in thirty minutes."

Standing up hurriedly. "Didn't you tell him I wasn't in the office?"

"I did, but he said for me to find you. He expects you to be here when he arrives. When I called back the housekeeper answered saying he wasn't on the property."

"Damn-it! Thirty minutes he said?"

"Yes."

Billie quickly cleared her desk grabbing her purse and keys.

"I'll drive into Amarillo for the rest of the day. Advise him, you attempted to call him back. I'll contact him tomorrow."

"Billie, you..."

The buzzer to the door stopped their conversation and Billie's movement. A couple entered the building.

"Who are these people?"

"It's your two o'clock appointment," Penny said.

Billie closed her eyes. The phone call from Leroy meant there would be some type of confrontation when he arrived. The old bastard seemed to be improving instead of deteriorating. She hoped he was lying about the location and arrival time. Her purse and keys were returned to their original place.

"Send them in. I'll attempt to get this completed quickly so I can leave."

Penny nodded showing the couple to Billie's office. She checked her watch as ten minutes increased to twenty. The couple continued to ask ridiculous questions in regards to a simple contract. Explaining each time the paperwork was safe to sign. Standing the moment her secretary ushered them out the door reaching again for her purse when the front door opened. Jackson walked inside heading straight for her office.

She met him at the door. "Jackson, I don't have time to talk with you. I'm heading to Amarillo," she said, pushing past him walking towards the back door.

"What about Leroy?" he asked.

Billie stopped, turning around. "Leroy?"

"Yes. Blessan contacted me at the courthouse asking me to meet him here. She's very worried about him," Jackson said.

"Worried?"

"She said his health drastically changed for the worse since his return from Houston. The treatments didn't seem to have benefited him as the doctor had hoped."

"I didn't know," she said walking up to Penny's desk.

"Well, you might have known if you'd return Blessan's phone calls. She's very upset. Is it true you haven't contacted her to check on him? This type of behavior is beneath you, Wilhelmina."

Billie's face turned red. She began to respond, then hesitated when Penny began pointing towards the door.

"I've been busy, Jackson. He is not my only client," she said.

Jackson heard Leroy's truck.

"If what Blessan said is true, Leroy shouldn't be driving. I can't believe he was forced to come into town because you won't pick up the damn phone. I'm going to go see if he needs help. The least you can do is open the door for him."

Billie was breathing hard from Jackson's accusations. She waited at the door as he assisted Leroy out of the truck. Blessan was correct. Leroy was pale and his clothes were hanging on him. He looked terrible. She smiled. Penny stepped forward opening the door.

"I'll see you at Lynn's when you're finished," Jackson told him.

"Thank you, buddy. Hello Billie, Penny."

"Come in, Leroy," Billie said.

She backed up allowing Penny to assist him in the door. The two of them walked into her office. Leroy turned, shutting the door which surprised her.

"Were you going somewhere?" he asked pointing at her purse.

She didn't answer him. "Any particular reason you shut my office door?"

"I don't want the whole town to know my business. Your secretary doesn't keep secrets very well."

"Can I get you anything to drink?" Billie asked sitting down behind her desk.

"Wilhelmina, what you can get me is the damn papers for the sale of my ranch to Blessan Hackney. It has been almost three months! If I had known this was going to take you this long, Jackson would be doing it!"

"Leroy, you are invested in more than just the ranch. You know these things need to be done correctly, it takes time. I don't want to miss anything."

"Miss anything? You mean like your interest in an empty safe or all the appraisers you've paraded through the house. You are being ridiculous there isn't anything in the house except a bunch of old paintings and some dusty books I bought at a garage sale years ago. Get off your butt and do the job you've been hired to do!" He grabbed the edge of her desk coughing violently.

Billie stood up. "Leroy, let me get you some water."

He held up his hand. "I'm fine. I want this done in the next thirty days or I will find someone else. My time is limited. Do not make me regret hiring you."

"I'll have it ready," she said.

"I expect you to bring the papers to the ranch," he said and stood up steadying himself on the chair.

Billie opened her office door following Leroy out. She watched as the frail man left her building and slowly drove away. Penny walked up to Billie.

"He looks terrible."

"Yes. Yes, he does. How long will it take you to have the papers ready on the sale of the ranch?" Billie asked.

"I've been working on it. I could have them ready before I go on vacation in two weeks."

"I forgot about your vacation. No hurry. You can finish it when you get back," Billie said.

"Are you sure?"

"Yes, things will be fine until you return."

Chapter 16

Medical Advice

It was a cool Saturday morning for June when Billie opened the back door of her office. It was unusual for anyone to be in the office on weekend but Leroy's physician refused to speak with her during his office hours. He agreed to a weekend call this morning to answer questions. Penny would return Monday and this was not the type of information to be shared with Glenmore.

Since Leroy's visit, she called Blessan every day to check on his health. In their conversations continual reassurance was given the paperwork for the sale of the ranch would be completed on time. The truth was she hoped each call would be greeted with Leroy has passed.

An official prognosis was needed on Leroy's condition. Collectors and interested buyers were becoming disenchanted with the continual postponement of the auction. Blessan and Jackson were not doctors and she wanted definite answers. It had taken five calls and an hour wait before he acknowledged her. Billie was not accustomed to such treatment when making a request. The stakes were high so if paying for long-distance charges was what it took so be it. He was hesitant at first to discuss any information regarding his patient. Billie pulled the I'm his attorney ploy to push the point of a necessary call. The phone rang as she filled her cup with coffee.

"Wilhelmina Walsh."

"Good morning, Dr. George Harmon. I do not have time for a lengthy conversation Mrs. Walsh, please make this quick. What can I do for you?"

"Thank you, for calling me. As I indicated to you earlier in the week, I am the personal attorney for Leroy Grinder. He has asked to have some papers drawn up for the sale of his property. My concern is whether he is competent to make this type of a decision."

She waited as there was a long pause before he began to speak.

"Mr. Grinder has a complicated prognosis. His treatments in Houston were experimental, with a disappointing outcome for both of us. I am surprised he is still alive."

"This information will be devastating for our little community," she said.

"I would suggest any legal matters be completed with haste."

"Thank you," she said hanging up the phone.

Billie smiled leaning back in her leather chair. Walking out to Penny's desk to locate the paperwork for the sale of the ranch. She took the file back into her office running it through the shredder. Picking up her purse heading towards the back door the office phone rang. She stopped to listen to the message being left.

The voice on the line was trembling. She could hear sniffing.

"Billie, this is Blessan Hackney. Mr. Grinder has been taken to Amarillo by ambulance. Please call when you get this message."

Billie walked over erasing the message.

"Oh, I'll call, first thing Monday morning."

Chapter 17

Blindsided

Blessan drove up to the main house with Shephard sitting in the front seat. It was Thursday and the men would expect their checks in the morning. She entered the house walking down the hallway to the library with her companion close by. Normally this was the time spent talking with Leroy. They discussed bonuses, time off, and possible terminations for poor job performance. She was extremely proud of the way the men worked together in his absence. In the last three weeks, the only serious discussion was with Shephard.

She guessed Billie felt it was no longer necessary to contact her once Leroy was sent to Amarillo. A week later he was transferred back to Houston where his condition worsened. Making the obligatory calls to her office became monotonous receiving the same apology each time.

"I'm sorry Blessan. Mrs. Walsh is out of the office, but I'll see she receives your message.

A ranch foreman's responsibility was to the land and men, but the uncertainty of this situation was never far from her thoughts. Thankfully, Jackson traveled to Houston with Leroy and continued to update her daily.

Before Leroy left they discussed the reasons for Billie's delay in the sale. He would smile, reassuring her things were progressing as they should on this matter. The door creaked as Guadalupe entered the library bringing a tray of food placing it in front of her.

"Miss Blessan, you need to eat."

"I will."

Guadalupe took a treat from her pocket giving it to Shephard. The housekeeper rubbed the dog's head speaking in Spanish to him. The payroll was completed, taking time to look over requests for time off while finishing the sandwich and a glass of milk. Guadalupe reentered the room.

"I didn't realize I was so hungry. Thank you, it was delicious."

"Miss Blessan."

"Yes."

"The sheriff is at the front door asking for you."

"The sheriff? She looked at the small clock on the desk. "At this time of the evening?"

"Yes, Miss Blessan. He has some papers for you."

"What kind of papers?"

"He did not tell me. Miss Blessan, there are five deputies with him. They have trucks and trailers with them."

She stood up walking to the front door where Sheriff Joe Howard stood with several deputies. His five-star badge with Sheriff written on it glimmered in the lights of the porch. Shephard appeared at her side.

"Blessan, hello Shephard."

The dog wagged his tail.

"Sheriff Howard. It's a little late for a social call. Has something happened to one of my ranch hands?"

Turning his head towards the deputies then back to her. "I need to come inside. This isn't something to discuss on the front porch."

"Of course." She turned to Guadalupe who was standing behind her. Coffee in the library, please."

"Yes, Miss Blessan."

Shephard led the way back down the hallway to the library. Guadalupe entered behind them with coffee and cookies.

Leaning down to the dog. "Come, Shephard, Guadalupe has warm tortillas in the kitchen."

Shephard followed her out closing the door.

The sheriff removed his hat running his fingers through his black thick hair. "Blessan, I have papers signed by a judge removing you, the housekeeper, and all the men from the property."

She smiled. "This is a joke."

The sheriff shook his head handing the papers to her. "I wish it were."

Blessan was stunned, sitting down to look through the paperwork.

"Who did this?"

"Wilhelmina Walsh. She filed for control of the ranch and all assets in Leroy's absence."

Blessan lowered her head, trying to understand how Billie could move so quickly obtaining complete control.

"Who's going to take care of the ranch?"

"I asked her the same question."

"Did she give you any kind of an answer?"

"She said for me not to worry about the ranch. There would be arrangements made later in the week."

"Sheriff, we have cattle out here, a lot can happen in a week," Blessan told him.

"I explained all of this to her. The only thing she was concerned about was the house. The cows could fend for themselves."

"The house is her main concern?"

"I am to collect all keys to every building on the property. The house is to be locked, no one will be allowed inside except her. It will remain like this until Leroy comes back home or..."

"Or dies. Leroy didn't expect his secret to be kept forever. Is there any possibility this could wait until morning? I need to explain the situation to the men and Guadalupe?"

"Unfortunately, the papers say immediately. No one is to touch or take anything except personal property."

"Sheriff it's payday. My men will receive their money."

He nodded. "Do what you must, leave the checkbook."

Blessan rubbed the back of her neck. "Give me a moment." She picked up the phone making a call to the bunkhouse. "Ralph, I need everyone to the main house now." Hanging up the phone she looked across the desk.

"What are you thinking, Blessan?"

74

"Sheriff, this might take a while. My men have horses, tack, personal items. I assume that's why your men are here with trailers."

"I came prepared with two trailers and the trucks. If we have to make several trips, so be it. My deputies are here to help you and the men. Why didn't you or Leroy explain the situation out here?"

Closing her eyes, then staring at the ceiling. "Not his way to bother others with a personal problem. You've been his friend long enough to know who he is."

"I had no idea she planned to do this or I'd have given a heads up. Billie went around all of us, didn't even use a local judge."

Blessan picked up the papers. "Judge Smith would never have signed this."

"No, he wouldn't have and that's the reason she drove into Amarillo. None of us like this, but my hands are tied legally."

"Leroy's trust and faith in Billie has been unwavering. I never believed anything like this would happen," she said.

"There is one item I was advised, no let me rephrase this. She demanded I personally take possession of."

"What would that be sheriff?"

"She wants the keys and combination to Leroy's safe."

Blessan shook her head. "Sheriff, I do not have the combination or the keys to the safe."

"Who does?"

"Leroy is the only one who knows the combination. Jackson Hellman has the keys."

The sheriff smiled for the first time since arriving at the ranch. "Well, I guess she can drive to Houston and pick them up personally."

"It won't matter, if she doesn't have the combination there is no way to open the door. I don't understand her obsession with the safe. Leroy and I have both told her there is nothing of value inside of it."

"Billie doesn't believe either of you. She told me no one keeps an empty safe and is determined to open it."

The knock at the door interrupted the conversation. Guadalupe, Shephard, and ten men entered the library.

He stood putting on the hat. "I'll be outside. Pay your men and explain the situation."

"Thank you. Guadalupe, you need to remain, please."

Everyone in the room remained silent until the door was closed.

"Mr. Grinder's situation has become critical. We are to vacate the ranch immediately, please take only your personal property. The deputies outside will help with the horses. Guadalupe and I will lock up the house."

"What about our pay?" Ralph asked.

Blessan pointed to the envelopes on the desk. "I've got all of you taken care of for now."

"Where will we be going, Miss Blessan?" Guadalupe asked.

Blessan smiled. "A safe place. Guadalupe, will you wait for me in the kitchen?"

"Yes, Miss Blessan."

"Ralph, please take charge of the men so we can get this done quickly."

"Yes, boss."

She watched as Ralph left, followed the men.

"Lee, I need for you to remain for a few moments."

"Yes, boss."

When the two of them were alone she motioned for him to sit down.

"Does your brother still live in Amarillo?"

"Yes."

"I have a favor to ask. Please know you are not obligated to help me though it would be greatly appreciated. You'll be helping Mr. Grinder."

"Yes, ma'am. If it will help you or Mr. Grinder, anything."

Twenty minutes later Lee left the house to join the others. Blessan entered the kitchen where Guadalupe was boxing the perishable food items to take with them.

"I hadn't thought about the food."

"I'll not allow this to go to waste, or be left for that woman."

"Did you call your husband?"

"Yes, Miss Blessan. My family will be waiting for us."

She and Shephard walked through the house one last time, turning lights out when exiting each room. Entering the kitchen Sheriff Howard was helping Guadalupe with the last box of food.

"You aren't going to tell her about the food, are you?" Blessan teased.

He laughed shaking his head. "Are you and Shephard finished checking the house?"

She looked down at the dog who began to whine. "We're all done."

"Blessan, again, I'm sorry."

"Sheriff, don't worry. We have a place to go," she said handing him the keys to the ranch.

Joe Howard watched as Blessan drove away with Shephard standing in the back of the truck. He locked the back door walking out the front seeing the tail lights of her truck disappear. Before locking the front door he stared at the keys.

"Damn you, Wilhelmina."

Chapter 18

Going Home

The drive from the Circle G to the other side of town gave Blessan time to think. She would need to make a tentative plan for herself and the men until this issue was resolved. Smiling when the truck entered through a gate she knew well following the road up to the barn. The two trailers from the Sheriff's office appeared to be finishing with a first-run from the ranch. Several of the men shook the deputy's hands before they left to go back for the rest. Ralph walked up to the truck.

"How many are left to come?" she asked.

"Three more," Ralph answered.

"I'll be out when everyone is here."

"Yes, Boss." He said walking away.

Checking her watch it was one in the morning. Evicting someone from their home in the middle of the night proved what she already knew. Greed and control overcame any sense of humanity or caring for the people Billie represented. Guadalupe exited the pickup followed closely by Shephard, entering the house with her. When she returned to the truck both daughters were with her. Maria was thirteen and Mary, fifteen, both girls dressed ready to help.

She smiled at them. "Good morning girls."

"Hello Miss Blessan," they said.

"Girls, take the boxes inside the house put away the food."

"Yes, Mama," they answered.

"Mary, did you put clean sheets on Miss Blessan's bed?"

"I did as you asked."

"You didn't need to worry over me. I can sleep in the barn. It's unfair to displace your family when I no longer live here," Blessan said.

"Oh no, you will sleep in your home and bed. I'll have something cold for you to drink inside," Guadalupe said.

Blessan knew it would do no good to argue when Guadalupe made a decision. "I can't thank your family enough."

"No. It is us who thank you every day. Tell my boys they are needed inside."

She nodded walking out to the barn where the men and Hector were settling the horses in stalls. The boys placed fresh hay they managed to bring from the Circle G for the horses. Hector Jr. was seventeen, Diego just turned ten.

"Hector, you and the boys are needed inside. I'll be there in a few minutes."

"Si Miss Blessan." He turned to his two sons motioning for them to go.

She turned to her men. "Is everyone here?"

"Still missing three, but I can pass on the information," Ralph said.

"I can't say for positive how long we'll be out here, but you will be paid, fed, and have a place to sleep. Tomorrow we'll set up some showers out here it won't be fancy but will wash the dirt off all of you. It will take me a couple of days to make arrangements for toilets so take it out far away from the house," she said.

"The men want to know what are we going to do," Ralph said.

"There are repairs which need to be done to the barn and house. There are fences down, please find and repair them. A full day's work will be expected from everyone. One last thing, Guadalupe's boys will be around helping you be decent and mindful of your language."

"Can we go to town tomorrow night?" Lee asked.

Blessan looked at all of them. "Take your pay, go to town but be back here Sunday night ready to work Monday. Any man not here at seven will no longer have a job. I need all of you, Leroy needs you, understood."

"Yes boss," they all said.

The trailer with the last of the men and animals pulled up to the barn. "Ralph, get everyone settled. I will need the men who cook to help Guadalupe and the girls with meals. Get some sleep and stay out of jail in Amarillo."

She turned walking out of the barn. After the last few hours, the men could use two days off. Entering the back door of the house into the kitchen Guadalupe's daughters had finished putting away the food. The two boys came through stopping long enough to take a box of beer with them out to the barn.

"The men will appreciate a cold drink," Blessan said.

"I figured they needed something," Guadalupe said.

"I have given everyone two days off, so your boys won't have to put up with their roughness."

"Thank you, Miss Blessan, but our boys will be fine."

Hector walked into the kitchen sending his daughters to their brothers' room. Guadalupe set a plate of sweet bread on the table with a glass of tea. The three of them sat down.

"I'll make calls to the grocery, feed, and hardware stores in the morning. Hector speak with Ralph to figure out what will be needed for the horses for at least a month. Guadalupe, the two men who cook at the bunkhouse will be expected to help you. We are feeding seventeen people three meals a day. My men are being paid to work so keep them busy with all the repairs which need to be done, including the house.

"Could we paint the house?" Hector asked.

She smiled. "Anything you need or want, maybe its time for that additional bedroom."

"Another bedroom would be helpful. It's been some time since you were here to visit," Hector said.

"It is nice to come home even for a little while," Blessan said.

"Why did that terrible woman do this to Mr. Grinder and all of us?" Guadalupe asked.

"Greed."

Hector crossed himself. "She will only find an empty purse."

"I'm going to take my bread and tea to the bedroom."

"I placed clean towels in the bathroom," Guadalupe said.

She left the kitchen where Hector and Guadalupe were making a long list of needed items. A moment later Blessan was standing in the shower watching the dust of a terrible day wash away. A familiar pair of pajamas was found on the bed, recently washed and folded. Lying on the bed leaning back taking in every corner of her old room. Feeling guilty for not coming back more often to make repairs and seeing to the land. At least now there was the manpower available to accomplish it.

The Hernandez family had been good stewards of the property for almost eight years. Blessan was fortunate to have found them. As a ranch foreman at the Circle G, she was required to be available at all times. It was impossible to run two ranches. Smiling she knew they were taking care of the ranch, raising their family, and making new memories.

The smell of fresh sheets took away some of her worry for the Circle G. Finishing the tea and bread, making a mental note to call Jackson tomorrow. He needed to be informed of Billie Walsh's actions. Blessan would trust him to make the right decision with Leroy.

Chapter 19

Responsibilities

Billie took a few days off to allow the news of the Circle G eviction to settle among the gossips in town. She usually ignored the diner talk, but this time it was different. Leroy was not a stranger and Blessan was the favorite daughter of the town. His death will leave a path to unbelievable riches, and a new life far from the Texas panhandle. It was a relief to know Jackson would not be adding fuel to everyone's conversation in town. He remained in Houston at Leroy's side. This morning she parked the Range Rover behind her building entering through the back door.

"Good morning!"

Penny jumped grabbing her chest.

"Good Lord Billie, you scared me to death."

"I parked out back today. I've received some unpleasant messages left on my phone machine at home. I expected a few people to be upset but the profanity is too much," Billie said.

"Oh Billie, I am so sorry to hear you're being harassed. It's just small-town talk it will settle down in a few weeks. You should just ignore it."

"Penny, you know my only concern is for Leroy. It's for the best."

"I know it is, Billie. Leroy needed someone with a firm head on their shoulders to make the right decisions."

"Have there been any calls from Blessan?" Billie asked.

"No. You have an appointment in about thirty minutes with Randall Ingles. He owns a company called Ranch Rounders."

"Wonderful, he comes highly recommended to care for property in these situations."

Billie turned shocked at the mess on her front window and began to point. "What is this?"

"Eggs. Yesterday it was tomatoes, the day before..."

"Did you call Sheriff Howard?"

"I did, Billie. I've made a report each day. The window service should be here anytime."

"This is not acceptable! Vandalism, all because someone is unhappy with my actions. I'm required to do what is in the best interest of my client."

"It's probably kids who have heard their parents complain," Penny said.

"I'll make another call to the sheriff to ask for an increase in nightly building checks. Any issues with your car or house?" Billie asked.

"No. It's all focused here."

"The behavior of this town is juvenile."

"Please ignore it, Billie."

Walking into her office, angry and upset with the small-minded town mentality. She picked up the phone dialing Joe Howard's office.

"Sheriff's office, Lucretia speaking."

"Wilhelmina Walsh to speak with Sheriff Howard."

"Just a moment."

"Joe Howard speaking."

"Billie Walsh here."

"Billie, I am not in the mood to hear about the mess at your office. What did you expect?"

"I didn't expect to have profane messages or the need for a daily window cleaning."

"You stepped in it this time. Blessan and Leroy aren't strangers."

"Joe, I haven't done anything to Leroy except look out for his best interest."

"There aren't a lot of people in town who see it that way. Why did you have them evicted in the middle of the night? It was close to midnight before we could get everyone off the property."

"I have a responsibility to make sure everything at the ranch is kept as Leroy wants it. What guarantee do I have Blessan or those ranch hands won't steal him blind while he's gone?"

"Good God, Billie, do you hear yourself? Bo and Gean were your best friends, you've known Blessan since she was born. Old Ralph is Amos's cousin. Don't you think if there was going to be an issue it would have been before now? You are being ridiculous!"

She looked up as a tall man entered the office.

"Joe, I do not wish to argue about the way I do my business. I expect you to do yours, please have more patrols around my building during the night. I want this mess stopped."

"I'll do what I can."

"I have another question."

"I'm sure you do," he said.

"Why weren't the keys to the safe and combination in the envelope you left me? Where are they? I told you to make sure she gave them to you."

"Jackson has the keys and the one person alive with the combination is Leroy Grinder. You'll have to get it from him. If I were you I wouldn't wait too long," Joe said disconnecting.

Billie closed her eyes. If he has a Renoir, there could be anything in the safe. Diamonds, a Fabergé egg, something of great value was locked inside, she was sure of it.

"Billie, a Mr. Randall Ingles to see you," Penny announced.

She stood up to shake hands with him.

"What can I do for you Mrs. Walsh?" he asked.

"You come highly recommended from an associate. I understand you have some experience in this type of situation?"

Penny entered the office with coffee.

"Thank you."

"Billie, can I get you anything?"

"No. Please close the door.

He waited until the door closed.

"If you are speaking of a forced eviction with a hostile takeover of property, yes. The herd and property size will determine the number of men I will call to work the ranch. Is there a bunkhouse on the property or will we be staying in the main house?"

"No! No one is to be allowed inside the house except me. I understand there is a fully functioning bunkhouse," she said.

"I need you to understand my men will handle the cattle, nothing else. We do not mend fences or harvest crops. Food, feed for our horses, gas, are all extra on top of my standard fee. Do you have any idea how long this will take?"

"Once I have verification of death, which should be very soon. I believe four to six weeks."

"I need the keys and directions."

Billie removed an envelope from the desk handing it to him. He took out the small map of the property.

"How many men did he have running the ranch?

"Ten men with a foreman."

"I'll need two thousand now to get settled."

"Two thousand seems a little steep for food and feed," she said.

"The ranch is how far from town?"

"An hour maybe more."

"I have no idea if there was food left. A dozen hungry men can't live on an empty pantry. The horses will need to be fed, too."

Billie pressed the intercom. "Penny, bring the checkbook in here please."

"Right away."

She took a check from the register handing it back to Penny. Filling in the amount then handing it to him.

"Thank you," he said, placing the folded check in his shirt pocket.

"Penny will have a check waiting for you every Friday morning until you are no longer needed."

Randall stood up. "I appreciate simple jobs. If I need extra cash?"

"If you should need additional money inform Penny."

Billie leaned back in the chair smiling as he left the building. This was one less issue to deal with allowing her to focus on the job ahead. The overwhelming desire to begin an inventory of the artwork would need to be restrained for now. Once she received word Leroy was dead the work could begin. She would continue to be the strong caring guardian in public view concerned with her friend and client.

Chapter 20

Loss

A month had passed since Billie obtained control of the Circle G. Randall arrived every Friday at ten picking up a check. Reporting all was quiet, cattle tended to and no issues since their arrival. To his surprise, the ranch bunkhouse and barn were well stocked. After the initial report on the situation at the ranch, she felt the two-thousand dollar check should have been returned. He checked the exterior of the main house daily to be sure no one tampered with the locks or damaged the windows.

The vandalism at the office ceased with no one arrested or charged. Since the eviction of Blessan from the ranch, the business at her office drastically decreased. The clerk at the courthouse was no longer calling with the information she counted on for easy money. Confronting her, Billie was informed a list is now being followed allowing an equal opportunity for all attorneys to these cases. It appeared the town was not convinced of her sincerity for Leroy.

Billie considered another call to Leroy's physician but knew Jackson would insinuate she was circling the prey. Walking out to Penny's desk she was shocked to see her playing solitaire.

"Do I have any appointments?"

"Nothing today," Penny answered.

"I am going to go out to the ranch to check on the house. It's been a month."

"Do you mind if I close the office around two? I have an appointment with Flo." Penny asked.

"You can leave now if you'd like," Billie responded.

Walking back to get her purse and keys she headed to the back door when the phone rang. Penny began to snapping fingers motioning for her to wait.

"Okay, I'll tell her," Penny said hanging up the phone. "Billie, I think you should stay here."

"Who was on the phone?"

"Jackson, he's on his way. He said for you not to go anywhere and wait for him."

"This has to be about Leroy."

She walked back into her office straight to the credenza behind the desk. Leaning over pulling out a bottle of scotch. Jesus Christ, the old bastard took long enough to die. She poured a drink.

"Celebrating?"

Turning to face Jackson standing in the doorway of her office.

Penny stood behind him. "Billie, I'm sorry he came in the back door."

"It's fine Penny. Come in Jackson, drink?"

"I'll have the Glenlivet your drinking, not the cheap watered down crap you give new clients."

Billie handed the bottle to him.

"Help yourself." She sat down behind the desk.

Jackson took the bottle picking up Billie's coffee cup from the desk. He emptied the cold coffee in the wastebasket pouring himself a drink.

"I know what you've done, Wilhelmina, and why. Leroy told me before he died last week."

Billie stood up. "Last week, why didn't someone inform me? I am his attorney and should have been notified immediately!"

"I'm notifying you now. He was cremated per his wishes. I have given his ashes to Blessan along with the death certificate."

"She has no right to the death certificate just as you have no right to the safe keys."

Jackson looked over the top of the coffee cup smiling.

"I will never give you those keys. They will do you no good without the combination."

"I guess I'll have it drilled open."

"Do whatever you want. It will take time to get his estate through probate."

"You forget who has all the information on his estate. I'll have it done in a week."

"The big payday you've been waiting for. If I were you, I'd leave town when this is over."

"Sounds like a good idea to me. Finish your drink and leave, Jackson."

He emptied the cup, picked up the bottle walking away.

She followed him to the door, locking it after he left. Leaning against Penny's desk she let out a sigh looking up at her.

"Billie, do you want me to call the sheriff?"

"No. He's all talk and is upset over the death of his friend. Why don't you go ahead and leave? I'll close up the office?"

"Are you sure, Billie?"

"I think we could both use a break after Jackson's visit. Put the phone on record and turn the lights off when you go. I'll be here for another hour."

Penny didn't waste any time leaving the office. Billie locked the front door and the back door. It was difficult to determine who deserved her anger at this moment, Jackson or the damn doctor in Houston. She should have insisted in their conversation the death certificate be sent directly to the office. Jackson's interference should have been expected, involving Blessan is his payback.

Billie hadn't spoken to her since the eviction. The sheriff didn't offer any information as to where everyone was now residing. She knew of one location where everyone could take refuge. Grabbing the Rolodex of phone numbers, thumbing through finding an old number. It had been over ten years since she dialed the number and wasn't completely sure it was still in order. The phone rang over ten times before finally being answered though no one immediately spoke.

"Blessan, this is Billie. I understand you have something which legally belongs to me."

"I see Jackson has been there. I'm surprised you still have my parents number."

"I figured the only place you could go would be that tiny three-bedroom ranch house sitting on a spit of land. I would imagine it wasn't in the best of condition when you arrived."

"We've made do out here no thanks to you. I am assuming if I didn't have the death certificate you'd never have contacted me."

"Let's make this as amicable as possible, shall we dear? I would prefer not to involve Joe Howard again. Come out to the ranch on Saturday alone."

"Saturday, what time?"

"Three." Billie disconnected, quickly made a call to the bunkhouse.

"Randall here."

"Your services are no longer needed. I want all of you off the property by Friday. I'll have a check waiting."

"Sounds good. I can't refund your money," he said.

"What money?"

"Sick animals out here needing to be seen and checked by the vet," he explained.

"It's fine. I need you gone."

"It's been a pleasure," he said and hung up.

Billie was concerned Penny didn't mention anything about additional expenses. Remembering she'd permitted Penny to write checks as needed. Taking a moment to find the checkbook and locate the additional cost.

"What is God's name could cost four thousand dollars?"

Wanting to be upset, until she realized it was a small price to pay for the success of her plan. The time was here, finally. One person was keeping her from obtaining an obscene amount of wealth. The law made it possible to obtain complete control of the Circle G. If Blessan refused to release the death certificate the law would be used again.

Though the question of why with all the vast wealth he accumulated a will was never prepared still perplexed her. It was a little late to speculate on his mistake, nor did it matter now. Stretching out both arms laughing as everything belonged to Billie Walsh.

Chapter 21

Celebrating Death
  Circle G. Ranch

Billie smiled at the gorgeous day driving out to the Circle G. She found it curious the stores in town hadn't placed black buntings outside. The mayor was silent, no declaration or proclamation for a week of mourning in Leroy's honor. Jackson may be involved in some manner keeping everything simple. The silence on his death was to her advantage really, making it easier to proceed with the plan. The entrance gate didn't seem to work well causing extra time to figure how to secure it. Pulling into the circle drive Billie took a moment to congratulate herself on how easy this had played out. The out-of-pocket costs were more but what was a few thousand when she would have millions to spend.

Grabbing the small ledger next to her it was time to inventory every sellable item in the house. She turned towards the back of the book, viewing her own to-do list. The realtor in Amarillo was progressing with the sale of the house in Glenmore. The estimated appraisal value was disappointingly lower than hoped, but living in a small town like this it was to be expected.

The office building would need to be sold or maybe not. Jackson indicated an interest when he thought she might leave town after Amos died. Typing a letter this morning, Billie instructed Penny to give the keys to him with her blessing. In the same letter, Penny was thanked for her years of service including a nice compensation check. The letter was placed in the center drawer of the credenza, where it would be found after she left town. Leaning into the leather seat, looking at the house.

"Mine! All mine."

Leaving the car she walked up the steps to the house taking the key opening the door. A warmth of richness filled every sense in her body with the first step on the hardwood floor. It was a wonderful feeling to have more money than Blessan Hackney or Ambrose Glenmore. Entering the small kitchen she pulled the handle on the refrigerator door allowing the small light to illuminate the room. A bottle of champagne was the only thing in it.

"I'll open you later to celebrate," she said out loud turning to admire the O'Keeffe.

Billie felt the darkness of the room was playing tricks as she began to desperately search for the light switch. It appeared the painting was no longer hanging on the wall. Once the lights were on it became obvious all the paintings had disappeared.

"What the hell is going on here?"

Running out of the kitchen and down the hallway, Billie's heart raced. She passed the empty location, where the antique bookcase once stood. Bursting through the double doors of the library, she grabbed the long curtains pulling them from the rods to the floor. The sun began to reveal the truth. The guns and Renoir were no longer in their places. Someone had robbed her!

"No, this was not happening!"

Walking behind the desk Billie sank into Leroy's leather chair. She was the only person with a key to the house which meant either Jackson or Blessan lied! The two of them would be in the county jail by evening for stealing all her treasures. Reaching for the phone it was time to call Joe Howard.

"I don't believe that phone works, Wilhelmina."

Billie stood up staring at the doorway, grabbed her chest, and fainted.

Chapter 22

Answers

Leroy Grinder rolled Billie across the library in the chair to his leather couch. He was thankful she had not fallen on the floor since he was alone at the moment. Moving her from the floor would have been a two-man job. Taking the ammonia capsule, breaking it under her nose he stepped back quickly. Billie's immediate response was to sit up flaying arms in every direction, coughing and spitting. When the dramatics ceased he handed her a glass of water.

"I must be dead," she said taking a drink.

"Nope and neither am I."

"What the hell is going on?"

He motioned for her to follow him towards the desk taking a moment to make sure she could stand.

"Take a seat. We have some time before Blessan arrives."

"I want to know what the hell you've done, Leroy?" Placing both hands on her hips.

"I haven't done anything. Have a seat," he said.

"I disagree! You've made a fool of me and I intend to sue you."

Leroy started laughing as he sat down behind the desk. "Sue me, you'll be lucky if Joe Howard doesn't lock you up once I tell him what you've done."

She took a seat facing him. "You seemed to have lost the gaunt appearance and put some weight back on since our last meeting."

He smiled. "A little high-quality theatre makeup and some contacts. I'm surprised you didn't recognize Amos' old clothes and boots. I believe you gave them to the church after he died."

"Damn you. Leroy, stop playing games "

He stood up, opening the safe throwing the focus of this plan on the desk in front of her.

Billie picked up the book, "The Town of Glenmore - City of Corruption." "Where in the hell did you get this?"

"A good friend of mine sent it to me three years ago. He also loaned me his expensive gun collection."

Billie's face turned red. Picking up the book waving it at him. "You're the one who has kept this from being released."

"It wasn't just me."

"How were you able to stop the release of this book for three years?" Asking him placing the book back on the desk.

"I made a call to your publisher. She was more than happy to wait once I explained all the lies you told them."

"What lies?"

"Jesus, do you hear yourself? I simply explained you are not the author of the book. You took another individual's work placing your name to it."

"You will never be able to prove that!"

"Billie, you know what type of person Gean was. Did you think there was only one copy of the manuscript?"

Her face went pale. "Why would a publisher in New York listen to you?"

"Your publisher, Broad World Press, was very interested in what I had to tell them."

"You are no one! I can tell them you're lying. Who do you think they will believe? An officer of the court or some senile old rancher?" she asked.

"The reason your publisher would listen to this old rancher is that my sister owns Broad World Press," Leroy said.

Billie fell back in the chair.

"Blessan said she was dead. You have no heir or family."

"You assumed my sister was dead. Your reference to her being a nun was correct. Her name is Bernadette Nunn. She is alive, happily married, and very successful."

"Leroy, you hated Ambrose Glenmore like most people in this town. Why do you care?"

"I care because this book will destroy the city, ruin Blessan and the Glenmore name. The manuscript should've been given back to her when Gean and Bo died. She searched everywhere for months trying to find it. All copies were going to be destroyed and the publishing contract canceled." Picking up the book. "This was never yours to keep."

"You sound like Amos. He was a fool, too. Once I opened the box and read Gean's manuscript it wasn't about who got hurt. I saw an opportunity to make enough money to pay off Amos' gambling debts and get out of town."

Leroy saw Ralph and Lee standing in the door while Billie ranted about Amos. He let her finish before acknowledging them.

"You can come in," he told them.

Turning to see Ralph Walsh coming inside with Randall Ingles. Why was he there?

"I heard what you said, Billie. The only reason Amos gambled was to try to win enough money to keep your fat ass happy. You were never satisfied with what he gave you," Ralph said.

"Ralph, you're nothing but an old drunk. What do you know?" Billie asked.

"I know he loved you until the day he died. Your constant complaining caused him to overeat, smoke and drink. You killed him," Ralph said.

"Don't you have a bottle somewhere to go crawl in?" she said then looked at Randall "I guess you're part of this, too? Where is all my money?"

Randall nodded his head. "I should introduce myself. I'm Lee Randall Ingles, been working for the boss for a while now. The money was put to good use for feed and repairs to the Hackney ranch."

"Damn you! Damn all of you!"

Leroy held his hand up. "Cattle all good?"

"Yes sir," Ralph said.

"Everyone is back settled in the bunkhouse," Lee said.

"Good, I'll be out later."

The two men turned and left the library.

"Why are you worried about the cattle? They never left here," Billie said.

"My men moved the cattle from the Circle G to the Hackney ranch. Since you believed they were being cared for here, there was no reason for anyone to check. We moved the entire herd during the night. Lee would go to the bunkhouse occasionally. He just happened to be there the day you made the call to cancel his contract."

"You seem to have been a few steps ahead of me," Billie said.

"It was necessary to stay ahead for all for this to work. An example would be once you removed everyone from the ranch the cattle needed to be taken care of, though you could have cared less. Lee's sister-in-law works for the clerk's office in Amarillo. He made a call to his brother, explaining the need for extra work. Once word was out you needed experienced cowboys, his sister-in-law made sure she was the first to contact you."

"What I want to know is how did you manage to do all of this in a few months by yourself?" she asked.

"A few months?" Jackson said entering the library.

"I should have known you'd be a part of all this. I'll add your name to my lawsuit and complaint to the sheriff."

"Lawsuit? Sheriff? Leroy, did she get into your whiskey?"

"I don't think she had time. The sight of an empty house seemed to have upset her," Leroy answered.

Jackson held up the bottle of Glenlivet. "Why don't you relax and have a drink. This entire project was not a passing thought, Wilhelmina ."

"Why would I want to sit here and listen to the two of you?" Billie asked, standing up.

"Fine, you are free to leave. You might want to think about how you are going to explain all of this to Joe Howard. An empty house with millions of dollars" worth of artwork gone."

"I can see an issue since you are the one controlling the keys," Jackson added.

"You have forgotten all of the bills and appraisals you sent to me for payment. If you wish to continue your threats I will gladly disappear as Blessan has my ashes and death certificate," Leroy said.

"I hear St. Augustine is nice," Jackson said winking at Leroy.

"It's like I said, the sheriff will lock you up while Jackson and Blessan stand on the other side of the bars smiling. I'll be drinking rum punch with Lillie."

Billie looked at Leroy turning to face Jackson. She returned to the chair.

"Fine, pour me a drink."

"Gladly," Jackson said.

Chapter 23

Slipping Away

The last time Billie felt so much anger was after Amos's funeral. Ivan McMinn dared to present her dead husbands' gambling marker at her home. Reaching for the empty glass she held it out for Jackson to pour a drink. He simply smiled placing the bottle in front of her. The bottle was opened emptying the remainder.

She placed the full glass on Leroy's desk. "Sorry gentlemen, there wasn't enough to go around."

"No problem," Leroy said, stood, and walked to the table near the doors. He brought a bottle of Wild Turkey and two glasses. Pouring himself a drink then passing the bottle to Jackson.

"Before we get too deep into the liquor, I'd like to know how you managed all of this? You said a friend loaned the antique gun collection."

"Lester Haygood is the attorney in San Antonio who sent me the book. He is not only my friend but was close to Ambrose at one time. Lester helped write up the contracts everyone signed when they purchased the property in Glenmore."

"What does this have to do with anything?" she asked.

"When the book arrived three years ago I was at a loss on how to stop you. Never planning to include Blessan. When you placed your name on Gean's manuscript there wasn't a choice."

"I knew you weren't smart enough to do this alone," she said taking a sip of the Glenlivet.

"Blessan initially came up with the plan. It was not something we could complete overnight. Each detail had to perfect without question or suspicion." Jackson raised his glass.

"Are you saying everyone in town is involved in this scheme of yours?" she asked.

"Not everyone, there would be no way to keep something like this quiet. I would never involve Joe Howard or your secretary who hasn't kept a secret since you hired her," Leroy said.

"You have gone to a lot of trouble over a book which hurts no one but the Glenmore's," she said.

"The families who moved to Glenmore with promises of a better life from Ambrose would suffer," Leroy said.

"What do the citizens of Glenmore possibly have to do with any of this? Please explain," she said.

"This book was never meant to be published it was written as a threat to Ambrose," Jackson said.

"Ambrose. He's been dead for years. Stop screwing around and give me some damn straight answers!"

"Do you want to tell her, Leroy?" Jackson asked.

"You don't know? Amos didn't tell you did he?" Leroy asked.

"What does Amos have to do with this? What the hell are you talking about? Answer me!"

"Ambrose intended to reclaim all the land Glenmore was built on. This meant even the smallest plot of land where homes were built. Ranches with hundreds of acres, every business even the county courthouse was not immune. The only land he couldn't touch was mine and the Hackney ranch."

"What you are saying isn't possible," she said.

"I'd say you failed to read the contracts completely like the rest of us," Jackson said.

"It was a standard contract like any I've signed before."

"No, it isn't. Ambrose placed a repossession clause in every contract signed on land purchases." Leroy opened a drawer pulling out the paperwork on her office.

"How did you get this?" she asked.

"You aren't the only person with friends at the county clerk's office," Leroy said.

Jackson took the contract turning to page three pointing to a subsection so small it would be easily missed.

"It states the land, buildings or improvement will be returned, or forfeited anytime seller deems necessary," Leroy stated.

"This would never stand up in a court of law!" she said.

"You are possibly right. The problem is there are few individuals in town with money to fight the contract besides you. Most of the folks here would be bankrupt living in their car or truck. Joe Howard would be forcing friends and neighbors out of their homes," Leroy said.

"Sounds kind of like what you did to Blessan," Jackson said.

"Gean never meant for it to go any further than being sent to the publisher. It was intended to be insurance for the citizens of the town," Leroy said.

"Ambrose died two years after Gean and Bo, these contracts would be void," she said.

"Except the next section which states the contracts will revert to his living heir," Jackson said.

"Blessan," she said.

"Yes," Jackson said.

"Why didn't this happen?" She asked.

"Blessan stopped it, or rather we did," Jackson said.

"Gean was an intelligent woman who kept a ledger as a child of Ambrose's dirty dealings. When she discovered the clause in the contracts and his plan to repossess the land the book was written. He was furious when a copy of the manuscript was presented to him. What no one knew was he contacted Lester adding an addendum to his will. If the book was ever published the contracts would be called due," Leroy said.

"You set the destruction of Glenmore in motion," Jackson said.

"The city would turn into a ghost town with Blessan and Gean to blame," Leroy said.

"I don't give a damn who is to blame," she said taking a drink. "Leroy, I want to know how you were able to get your hands on the Renoir and O'Keeffe?"

Leroy took a moment to digest Billie's last comment. Shaking his head looking towards Jackson.

"We are talking about the destruction of the town, people's lives ruined, businesses closed. Your only interest is about a painting?" Leroy asked.

"Paintings," she corrected him.

Jackson poured Leroy more Wild Turkey. "I told you, warned you, she wouldn't give a damn about anyone," he said holding out a hand.

"You were correct." Leroy stood up taking a fifty-dollar bill from his wallet handing it to Jackson. "All of the artwork was a loan from two art galleries in New York. Bernadette is acquainted with the private owners who allow them to be displayed. They granted her a short time loan."

"What about the books? Who'd you scam to get those?" she said taking a larger swallow of the Glenlivet.

"I believe those were Bernadette's weren't they Leroy?" Jackson said.

"Yes. She is quite the collector."

"Your sister owns all of them?" she said.

"Yes."

"You see Wilhelmina, once Leroy explained your betrayal and deceit Bernadette was pleased to assist us. She wanted to help correct the situation in any way possible to avoid a lawsuit. The publicity of being conned would ruin her business."

"Jackson, you know I hate people who use my... my given name." She took another drink. "The doctor, what about him? He... he falsified a death certificate. What about all those experimental treatments?" She began slurring words.

"George is my physician, we have known each other long before I came to Glenmore. The time I spent in Houston was more of an extended vacation. The experimental treatments were back-to-back games of golf. It seems my ranch life has kept me physically fit all these years. His academic and soon-to-be-retired life has left him soft. I beat him every game."

"I'll have him arrested for signing a death certificate and he'll go to jail, lose his license. I've heard enough!" She stood up holding the desk for balance.

"Is there something wrong, Billie?" Leroy asked.

"I need...need the sheriff. I'll prove what you did to me. I want my money."

"What we did? Billie, you confiscated my property under false pretense. Placed your name on a manuscript someone else had written. Envy and greed have led you here."

"You're all going to pay. I'll make sure you never get out of jail," she said.

"Leroy, it appears Joe Howard is going to be busy arresting upstanding citizens."

"Guess so," Leroy said.

Billie grabbed her head. "Where is that bitch, Blessan?"

"I'm behind you," she answered.

Billie whipped around to see Blessan with her damn big dog, who was growling. "Where is the death certificate? Give it to me! I have to get to the clerk's office to file for, for..."

"Boss, do you know what she is talking about? Why would I need a death certificate for someone alive?"

Shephard took a protective stance in front of Blessan continuing to growl at Billie.

"Get your big nasty dog out of my way!"

Moving in what appeared to be an aggressive manner towards Blessan, Shephard never hesitated. He charged forward taking her to the floor. Drawing a final breath Billie looked up into the faces of Leroy, Jackson, Blessan, and that damn dog standing over her.

Chapter 24

Reborn

Leroy couldn't believe a full month had passed since his return to the ranch. The cattle roamed the land on the Circle G, and the cowboys found a greater appreciation for their job. The city of Glenmore was saved from a terrible fate. The Glenmore's and Hackneys would only be known for the good they did for the community. Business owners would have a livelihood and families a home for their children to grow up in. No one would know the price paid by a few.

Guadalupe brought her daughters to the ranch to help remove the darkness of Billie Walsh. His home was being transformed back into the light with a few simple aesthetic changes. Black curtains were removed, dark paneling was being replaced with drywall and light paint. The radio now played loudly in the kitchen accompanied by Guadalupe's singing each morning.

Leroy finished a letter placing it in an addressed envelope to his sister. He thanked her again for helping to right a wrong, asking her to visit the ranch. It was placed next to the one written to Lillie asking if it would be appropriate to see her in St. Augustine.

"Mr. Leroy," Guadalupe said from the door.

"Yes."

"The sheriff is here to see you."

"Bring some fresh coffee with two pieces of cherry pie."

"Yes sir," she said walking away.

"Cherry pie. You know my weakness," Joe said entering the library. He removed his hat shaking hands with Leroy.

"I figured you'd like to stay a bit and hear of my miraculous recovery," Leroy said.

"I'm just happy you're home and things around here are back to normal."

"What can I do for you, Joe?"

"I'm looking for Billie. Have you seen or spoken with her since you returned home?"

"No. I am considering some type of legal action against her. There was no cause for Blessan or my men to be treated in such a manner. I am thankful for the kindness you and your deputies showed them during that terrible time. I won't forget it."

"It was a damn disgrace, killed my soul to do it. You may have to stand in line on filing a complaint," Joe said.

"Really?"

"It appears Billie was scamming a great many people." Joe took a moment looking around the library.

"Is there something wrong, Joe?"

"Did you paint in here? It seems brighter than the last time. Where is the painting, your gun collection?"

"I was tired of that dark paneling along with those drapes. Decided it was time to brighten things up. Do you like it?"

"Interesting a little paint and curtains can make such a change," Joe said.

"The painting wasn't mine, my sister in New York sent it for me to enjoy for a short time. The gun collection belonged to an old friend in San Antonio. He's been out of the country for an extended period. I kept them for safety purposes until his return. Why, is there a problem?"

"Billie sold the gun collection to an individual who made a large offer on them to keep them from going to auction. She kept baiting him until he made the right offer. He sent a check for the total amount."

"Let me guess, she cashed the check," Leroy said.

"Correct. He is somewhat upset," the sheriff said.

"Is the money still in her account?" Leroy asked.

"I wish it were that simple. It seems she took his money and placed a large down payment on a home in Austin.

"She had no right to sell anything in my home nor file papers to take control of it."

"I have discovered she was doing a number of things just this side of legal, unfortunately, this one went way over the line this time. The collector filed charges and I have a warrant for her arrest."

"Do you have any leads?"

"Her Range Rover was found in Amarillo at the airport. The police found a couple of travel brochures for a place called Tahini," Joe said.

Leroy tried not to smile. He knew Jackson obtained brochures for Tahiti. "What about Penny?"

Joe began to laugh. "Penny isn't just a gossip, she's nosey. When Billie didn't answer her phone or come back to work she began snooping around in the office. Guess what she found?"

"Not a clue."

"Billie left an appreciation letter for Penny containing a compensation check. The best part of the letter was she gave Jackson Hellman the office with her blessing," Joe said and began to laugh.

Guadalupe brought in two large pieces of pie and fresh coffee.

"Thank you," Leroy said.

"Guadalupe your pies are the best in town. I can only compare them to Millie's. God rest her soul."

Guadalupe crossed herself. "Thank you, Senor Howard. I knew Miss Millie she was a wonderful woman. I'll be in the kitchen if you need me."

The two men stopped talking, eating in silence until their forks pinged on the empty plates.

"Joe, tell me again about Jackson owning Billie's office."

"I spoke with him today. He said the judge advised him to file the paperwork then give it to the clerk. He is debating whether to keep Penny."

"Can I have Guadalupe bring you another piece of pie, Joe?"

"No. I will take a piece to go."

Leroy walked to the library door calling for pie to go for the sheriff. Guadalupe returned with a full pie wrapped with foil placing it on the desk in front of the sheriff. Smiling he picked up the dish standing to leave.

"I can drop your letters off on my way home if you'd like."

"I appreciate it sheriff, but I'm driving into town tomorrow. I usually meet Jackson for breakfast. It sounds like we will have a lot to discuss in the morning," Leroy said.

"If Billie is arrested..."

"The answer is yes, I will press charges. She has done enough damage to this town."

Joe nodded his head as the two men walked to the front door out on the steps.

"I've always liked the way your house faces east, missing the hot west sun in the summer. It's going to be a nice evening," Joe said putting his hat on.

"Yes. Yes, it is."

"When I took over this office, Sheriff Morgan passed on some wise words. He said to take care of the people and they'll do the same. You will never know how hard it was to serve those papers on Blessan."

"It's in the past. No one is holding you in a bad light. It was your job. Like I said inside I appreciate you taking care of my people. Billie fooled everyone. Come back next week, the calf fries will be hot and the beer cold," Leroy told him.

Joe nodded. "I'll be here along with the rest of Glenmore."

Guadalupe walked out on the porch joining Leroy. They watched the sheriff drive away.

"Is everything alright, Mr. Leroy?"

"Of course, things are just fine."

"Will Miss Blessan be here for dinner?"

Leroy looked at his watch. "Not tonight. It's payday."

Chapter 25

Interesting News

Saturday morning Leroy drove into Glenmore, dropped by the post office first mailing two letters. His favorite parking spot in front of Lynn's was empty. Walking around the pickup he waved at Jackson sitting by the large window. Several men inside waved, greeting him with smiles and yells of glad you're still with us. It made him feel a little guilty as it was never meant for the whole town to believe he was sick.

"Morning, Leroy. It appears everyone is happy you are still kicking."

"Jackson."

An older waitress walked up with a pot of coffee filling his cup. She was wearing a pair of jeans, a T-shirt with Lynn's across the front, and boots.

"Lynn, bring another cup Blessan is on her way," Leroy told her.

"Oh good. It's been a while since I've seen her. Leroy, it's good to know you are well. You gave all of us a terrible scare. Rumors flying around town you were in a bad way. We were all praying for you at the church. Thank God he heard us." She said leaning down to hug him.

"Yes, prayers can be answered occasionally," Jackson said.

"Jackson, you're the type of friend we should all have. God Bless you and Blessan for being at his side through all of this," she said pouring coffee. "I'll be back when Blessan gets here."

Leroy picked up his coffee, took a drink smiling. "I hear you've become the owner of the Walsh building."

"Yep, funny how things work out sometimes. I just have to pay my taxes on time and the utilities, nothing else."

"What about Penny?"

Jackson looked down for a moment. "I had a nice long chat with her yesterday. She would like to stay on. No, that isn't correct. Let me rephrase this. She begged me to let her stay."

"But?"

"I explained we didn't need town gossip to do a proper job. The Hellman Law Office would have a good reputation. If I discovered any improprieties' she would be dismissed."

"Did she ask about Billie?" Leroy asked.

"There's Blessan, I want her to hear this too," Jackson said.

Blessan entered the restaurant and was met by several greetings from the patrons. She took a few moments to respond to them then joined the two men at the table. Lynn walked over, filling her cup.

"Good to see you, Blessan," she said.

"Hello, Lynn."

"Are you three ready to order?"

Jackson looked around the table.

"I think so," he said.

"Blessan, what can I get you?"

She smiled. "I think we'll all have your special."

"Okay, three specials coming up."

"Are we that easy to read?" Leroy asked.

"I'm buying this morning and the two of you haven't changed your order for breakfast in five years," Blessan said.

"I have some information to pass on from Penny at the office," Jackson said.

"You decided to keep her?" Blessan asked.

"With a couple of stipulations," Leroy said.

The conversation ceased as Lynn returned to their table.

"Here you go, three specials," she said passing out plates. Lynn walked off bringing back a basket of hot biscuits with a large bowl of sausage gravy. She refilled their cups with hot coffee and left.

"I have some interesting information from Penny in regards to Billie before she disappeared," Jackson said.

Blessan stopped eating and leaned in towards the two men. "I want to hear this."

"It appears Billie had been a little secretive those last few weeks before leaving town. Penny revealed the file for the sale of the ranch disappeared."

"Disappeared? When?" Blessan asked.

"Let me guess. When I was taken to Amarillo by ambulance."

Jackson nodded. "My guess is she shredded it. Penny discovered Billie planned to sell her home."

"I assume someone called the office," Leroy said.

Jackson laughed. "The realtor from Amarillo with an appraisal."

"Billie planned to leave Glenmore a rich woman. First, she needed to confiscate my home, land and sell everything that wasn't nailed down inside the house. The charges for her services would be largely due to my estate. Her creative invoicing would leave nothing for the court to distribute," Leroy said.

"Unfortunately, a bad bottle of Glenlivet stopped her hopes and dreams," Jackson said.

"Has Penny destroyed any of Billie's records?" Blessan asked.

"No. She left everything intact. I jimmied the locks on the desk and found all the appraisals. The letter from Christie's on the Renoir and O'Keeffe was quite enlightening. It will take me months to go through the files. I'll need to rent a storage building as everything will need to be kept for years."

"What about her personal ledgers?" Blessan asked.

"Well, I found two ledgers. One for regular business, appointments, court cases, mostly general information. The second book was her creative billing invoices to the court; no wonder the town had a deficit. The pages on you, Leroy were very interesting. She detailed every item in her charges and the money she would receive from the sales. The Circle G would be split and sold in five acres parcels. Billie never intended to see Blessan was given the option to buy your ranch intact," Jackson told them.

"Oh my God. How was she going to do all of this?" Blessan asked.

"She wouldn't need to be here for the land sales. It would be easy to hand off to a realtor once the acreage was plotted off," Leroy said.

Blessan motioned for Lynn. "I need a dozen burritos to go please with the check."

"I know those aren't all for you," Leroy said.

"I promised Lynn's stuffed burritos to the men before they head into Amarillo."

"It must have been a good week," Leroy said.

"Yes, boss it was."

Lynn brought two sacks to Blessan ten minutes later. She handed her two hundred dollars.

"I think this will cover everything."

Lynn leaned over hugging Blessan. "Thank you."

"Nice tip," Jackson said.

"Boss, I need to go. Ralph told me we were missing twenty head before coming to town. Pretty sure, I know where they are hiding, " she said standing up.

Leroy smiled. "I bet you do. Will you be in for dinner?"

"No. Please tell Guadalupe to drop something at the bunkhouse for me. It will be dark before I get in."

Leroy nodded and they watched her leave. The sound of a big engine caused them to smile. A moment later a large white pickup drove by with Shephard's head hanging out the window.

"Is that new?" Jackson asked.

Leroy smiled. "I believe it is."

"Good morning!"

"Sheriff, have a seat," Jackson said.

"Leroy, I need you to stop by the office before you head back to the ranch. I want to go ahead and make a report. I'd like to have all this finished, and ready for the judge on Monday."

"Of course, any news?" Leroy said.

"I received a call from the FBI this morning. It seems Billie has been the focus of an investigation for tax evasion," Joe said.

"Well, this is an interesting turn of events," Leroy said.

"Jackson, they first asked me to have you not touch anything."

"They're late," Jackson said.

The sheriff held up his hand. "I already told them how long you've been in the building. They are sending two agents from Amarillo here Monday morning. They asked you not to destroy anything and they would like to speak with Penny."

"Sheriff, I haven't had time to go through much in the office files. What I found in the desk will be given to them. I hope they take everything with them as it will save me a storage fee. I would like to prepare Penny for their arrival unless they advised against it," Jackson said.

"I don't see an issue unless you feel she might be involved."

"Penny? Involved in tax evasion with Billie." Jackson said.

Joe Howard started to laugh.

"Sheriff, what can I get you?" Lynn asked.

"One of your big cinnamon rolls with a tall coffee to go."

"Be back in a minute," she said.

He stood up as she returned handing her a ten. "Keep the change."

"It appears today is going to be a good one for Lynn," Jackson said.

"Why is that?" Joe asked.

"Blessan gave her two hundred dollars before she left," Leroy said.

The sheriff smiled. "See you in a bit Leroy."

A few moments after the sheriff left, Leroy and Jackson began to laugh.

"I can't wait for Blessan to hear about this," Leroy said.

"Yeah, me too. Leroy, I'd better go clean up some of the paperwork they aren't going to need. I want to prepare Penny so she doesn't have a breakdown and say the wrong thing."

"The only thing she might do is bore them to death with all the non-important gossip of the town," Leroy said.

Jackson stopped, thinking for a moment. "Maybe I will just let nature take its course then."

Leroy laughed. "I have a report to make then some things at the ranch require my attention."

"I hope you're talking about cold beer with hot calf fries." Jackson smiled.

"Next weekend I'll need some help cooking," Leroy said. He walked back to his pickup. On the way back to the Circle G he thought about Lillie. He would give his letter a few days to arrive in St. Augustine, then take a chance and call her. Hopefully, she'd be willing to make a trip to New York with him to see the sights. A smile grew across his face, after all this time she was still a beautiful woman.

Chapter 26

Settling Accounts

The voice of George Strait echoed down the dark dry cellar where Blessan stood with a rope and small flashlight. A few minutes later she blinked opening the door walking out into the beginning of a beautiful sunset. Removing a cold beer from the cooler in the back of the new white Ford F-150 pickup she decided to take a break. When Shephard continued barking the rope was released to him.

"Easy boy, no need to pull on it so hard."

She removed the Astros baseball cap, wiping the sweat from her forehead with the back of a plaid sleeve. Taking a moment to think of the last three years of planning. If even one part had gone wrong everyone could have gone to jail. The town of Glenmore would be in ruins with her family to blame.

Blessan would not forget the time on the Hackney ranch or the kindness of good people. The first two weeks were an adjustment for everyone.

"Good morning, Miss Blessan. You did not sleep well again last night," Guadalupe said handing a cup of coffee to her.

"Did I wake you?"

"When you left the house before sunrise," she said, adding flour to the large bowl.

"I thought an early ride might help."

"Did it?"

Blessan smiled. "Not really."

The back door opened and two of the men entered. "Good morning, Boss. "Morning, how is the grill working with the meals?"

"It keeps these two out of my kitchen," Guadalupe said with a slight smile.

"It works reall nice."

"I hadn't thought about an extra fridge or freezer, but they were needed. Is Ralph awake?" Blessan asked.

"Here, Boss." Ralph walked inside.

Guadalupe began speaking in Spanish, making a shooing motion towards them.

"Okay, cooks stay come outside with me Ralph." The two left the small kitchen walking out into the light morning sky.

"You were up early, Boss. It's a little risky to be out roaming alone before light."

"If I didn't know every square foot of this land you'd be right. How're the repairs?"

"Going good, the fences have all been fixed and tightened where needed. The barn is almost finished, we went ahead and put a new roof on it, cleaned up inside. If we have time maybe a coat of paint."

"Inside the house repairs?"

"Working on them," he said.

"I have supplies for the addition coming in a few days."

"Boss, we're all pretty handy with fixing things up, but..."

She held up a hand. "I've hired a crew to do the framing, plumbing, and electrical work. We can do the rest. This is the least I can do for this family helping all of us."

"It was a little rough the first week, now it feels as if we've always been here. I haven't heard a cuss word except in town on the weekends." He walked up and placed a hand on her shoulder. "Whatever happens, Boss. We'll make it work."

They had made it work. The past few weeks at the Circle G work and life returned to normal. There was less complaining from the cowboys and cohesiveness since settling back into the bunkhouse. Maybe it was the realization of the dire consequences if it had not been for the intervention of a few strong individuals.

Crushing the can it was thrown in the back of the truck. One last job left to finish. Taking the rope from Shephard she tied it to the trailer hitch. One whistle motivated the dog to find a place in the front passenger seat. The truck was placed in a forward motion with a careful eye on the rearview mirror until the item appeared from the cellar. Jumping out of the truck she grabbed another beer. A chain was pulled from the bed to the item on the ground.

"Let's see if this damn thing is worth the money I paid for it."

Using the new wench in the bed of the pickup it slowly pulled the package up over the end of the tailgate. Blessan opened the beer, joining Shephard and Willie Nelson for a twenty-minute trip to the back section of the ranch.

A couple of coyotes began to call to the moon as it rose over the canyon. Of course, Shephard joined in the chorus. Her men were in Amarillo dancing, cussing, and drinking too much, but they earned it this week. A cool breeze caused the hair on both arms to rise when she rolled up her sleeves.

Turning to the best friend any foreman could have. "Come on Shepard, let's do this. Are you ready, boy?"

Shephard responded with a short bark.

Smiling. "Me too."

The chain was removed. Blessan grabbed the rope wrapped around a bundle, stepping back quickly. In one swift move it hit the ground with a heavy thud. Shephard jumped back, growling.

"It's okay, boy. Come on."

Dragging the item around the truck with one hand, she dropped it next to a blue tarp. The bright light of the full moon meant no other illumination was necessary. Disappearing for a second, Shephard returned dropping a shovel at his owners' feet.

"Thank you."

The two of them pulled the tarp back revealing a deep hole. The body was pushed over the edge with her boot. Shephard took a guarded position growling, baring his teeth as if Blessan was still in danger.

"It's okay boy."

The first shovel of dirt hit the burlap shroud scattering like mice running from the light. The dog began to pull on her jean leg moving towards the truck. She realized something important remained inside. The only printed copy of her mother's book and original manuscript were thrown in the hole.

She would be forever grateful to Leroy's sister for assisting in this endeavor. A guarantee there were no other copies or evidence the story had ever been sent to the publishing company. There would always be a place to stay should Blessan decide to visit New York.

Moving to the edge of the grave again Shephard laid down. Kneeling next to him she smiled at this unexpected coconspirator. The moon cast a final glow on the wrapped body of Billie Walsh. Standing Blessan collected another shovel of dirt.

"Well counselor, it's for the best."

About the Author

Janet began writing in 2009 while still a full time travel nurse. She writes multiple genres from Historical fiction, to Paranormal Thrillers. Not to say she doesn't have a sense of humor. Her E-book You Just Can't will leave you smiling if not laughing.

She has short stories in two different anthologies. Tales of Texas III and Nothing Ever Happens in Fox Hollow. A recent publication of a poem in Upon Arrival: Transitions, is something new for her. She has become active with Tellables/Chatables with three stories which can be heard on Alexa.

She can be found in Fifty Great Writers you should be Reading published by The Author Show, as a winner for 2017 and 2018.

An over-all category Grand Prize Winner for Chatelaine in Chanticleer Book Awards added to the thirty-five awards for The Look for me Series. Twenty-six awards to date have been given to her Paranormal Mystery Thriller series.

She was a peace officer at one time, promoted to the rank of Sergeant and worked in a multi-city unit investigating questionable deaths and homicides.

Retired now living in her home on Galveston Island she spends the day sitting on the deck, writing, drinking good wine and listening to the breakers.

Additional Titles BY JANET K. SHAWGO

Multi-Award-Winning Historical Series Look for Me, Wait for Me, Find Me Again
Multi-Award-Winning Mystery/Thrillers Archidamus and Legacy of Lies
Ebook Comedy You Just Can't
Short Stories: Tales of Texas Volume III
Let the Grapes Grow
The Yellow Rose

Tellables/Chatables
Sweet Penny Valentines Box of Chocolates
Dark Bitter Joy Halloween Box of Chocolates
An Inconvenience

Nothing ever happens in Fox Hollow Anthologies
Book I
Mirror, Mirror
Book II
The Tree

Upon Arrival: Transitions Poetry
Mother and Me

You can connect with me on:
🌐 http://www.janetkshawgo.com